"You Look So Beautiful, Kiley."

He stepped just inside the door to take her in his arms and give her a soft, lingering kiss. "I'll be the envy of every man at the ball."

"I was just thinking something very similar about you and the women attending the ball," she said, smiling.

"Is the pony princess okay with staying at your folks'?" he asked, as he helped her with her evening wrap.

Nodding, Kiley picked up her sequined clutch. "I don't know who was more excited about her spending the night with them, Emmie or my parents. She has them wrapped around her little finger."

Josh laughed as he placed his hand to her elbow and guided her out to his car. "She has that effect on just about everyone. She's an adorable little girl."

"Thank you," Kiley said, wondering when and how she was going to tell him that Emmie was his daughter.

* * *

It Happened One Night
is a Texas Cattleman's Club: The Missing Mogul novel—
Love and scandal meet in, Royal, Texas!

* * *

If you're on Twitter,
tell us what you think of Harlequin Desire!
#harlequindesire

Dear Reader,

Being an author is normally a solitary profession and quite often, a lonely one. That's why I'm always thrilled to be invited to participate with other authors on a miniseries like the Texas Cattleman's Club. I not only get to work with some of the most talented authors in romance, I become friends with some of the nicest ladies anyone would ever care to meet. We always have so much fun lining out details for our characters and story lines. This time was no different and I'm sure it shows in this latest installment of the TCC series.

In book 6 of the Texas Cattleman's Club: The Missing Mogul, you'll learn that Josh Gordon and Kiley Roberts met one night three years ago under a bizarre set of circumstances. Now that their paths have crossed again, they discover that was not only a night that neither of them have been able to forget, it changed their lives in a way they could have never imagined.

It Happened One Night was one of those stories I hated to bring to a close and I sincerely hope you enjoy reading it as much as I enjoyed writing it.

All the best,

Kathie DeNosky

IT HAPPENED
ONE NIGHT

—

KATHIE DeNOSKY

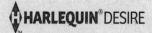

Special thanks and acknowledgment to Kathie DeNosky for her contribution to
Texas Cattleman's Club: The Missing Mogul miniseries

Recycling programs
for this product may
not exist in your area.

ISBN-13: 978-0-373-73283-8

IT HAPPENED ONE NIGHT

Printed in U.S.A.

www.Harlequin.com

KATHIE DeNOSKY

lives in her native southern Illinois on the land her family settled in 1839. She writes highly sensual stories with a generous amount of humor; her books have appeared on the *USA TODAY* bestseller list and received numerous awards, including two National Readers' Choice Awards. Kathie enjoys going to rodeos, traveling to research settings for her books and listening to country music. Readers may contact her by emailing kathie@kathiedenosky.com. They can also visit her website, www.kathiedenosky.com, or find her on Facebook, *www.facebook.com/Kathie-DeNosky-Author/278166445536145*.

This book is dedicated to the authors
of the Texas Cattleman's Club: The Missing Mogul.
Working with you all was a real pleasure.

Prologue

When Josh Gordon let himself into his girlfriend's apartment, he wanted two things—to make love to Lori and get some much-needed sleep. He'd spent a long day preparing job bids for Gordon Construction and an even longer evening wining and dining a potential client, who couldn't seem to make up his mind whether to give the contract for his new office building to the construction business Josh and his twin brother, Sam, co-owned or to one of their competitors.

Josh wasn't overly proud or happy about it, but they'd had enough to drink to float a fleet of ships before the man finally gave the nod to Gordon Construction. That's why Josh had made the decision to spend the night with Lori. The wine had dulled his normally sharp senses and he didn't think his being behind the steering wheel of a car was in anyone's best interest.

Since she had given him a key to her apartment a few weeks back and it was only a couple of blocks from the restaurant, walking to Lori's place had seemed wiser than trying to drive the five miles to his ranch outside of town. Besides, he hadn't seen her in a few days and missed losing himself in her soft charms.

The fact that their relationship was more of a physical connection than it was an emotional attachment should have bothered him. But neither he nor Lori wanted anything more, and he couldn't see any harm in two consenting adults spending their time enjoying each other for as long as the attraction lasted.

As he made his way across the dark living room and headed down the hall toward her bedroom, he decided not to turn on a lamp. The headache that had developed during the last few rounds of drinks already had his head feeling like his brain had outgrown his skull. The harsh glare of a light certainly wouldn't make it feel any better.

Loosening his tie, he removed his suit jacket as he quietly opened the bedroom door and, stripping off the rest of his clothes, climbed into bed with the feminine form he could just make out beneath the covers. Without thinking twice he took her in his arms and teased her lips with his to wake her.

He thought he heard her murmur something a moment before she began to kiss him back, but Josh didn't give her a chance to say more. He was too captivated by her. Lori had never tasted as sweet and the scent of whatever new shampoo she had used caused him to ache with the urgent need to sink himself deep inside of her.

When she ran her hands over his shoulders, then

tangled her fingers in the hair at the nape of his neck as she kissed him with a passion that robbed him of breath, a shaft of longing coursed through him. She needed him as badly as he needed her. He didn't hesitate to slide his hand down her side to her knee, then, catching the hem of her nightshirt, he brought it up to her waist. Never breaking the kiss, he made quick work of removing the scrap of silk and lace covering her feminine secrets and nudged her knees apart.

His heart felt like it might jump right out of his chest when he rose over her and she reached to guide him to her. Her desire for him to join their bodies was as strong as his and, giving them what they both wanted, he entered her in one smooth stroke.

Setting an urgent pace, he marveled at how much tighter she felt, how her body seemed to cling to his. But the white-hot haze of passion was stronger than his ability to reason and he dismissed his confusion as a result of too much wine.

When she clenched her tiny feminine muscles, he knew she was poised on the edge, and deepening his strokes, Josh pushed them both over the edge. As he emptied himself deep inside of her, her moan indicated that she was experiencing the same mind-blowing pleasure that pulsed through him, and feeling drained of energy, he collapsed on top of her.

"Oh, Mark, that was incredible."

Josh went completely still as his mind tried to process what he had heard. The woman he had just made love with had called him Mark. If that wasn't enough to send a cold sense of dread knifing through him, the fact that it wasn't Lori's voice sure as hell was.

What had he done? Where was Lori? And who was the woman he had just made love with?

Sobering faster than he could blink, Josh levered himself to her side, then quickly sat up on the side of the bed to reach for his discarded clothes. "I…um… oh, hell. I'm really sorry. I thought…you were Lori."

The woman was silent for a moment before she gasped and he heard her jump to her feet on the other side of the bed. "Oh, dear God! No, this can't be… We didn't… You must be—"

"Josh," he finished for her, since she seemed to be having problems conveying her thoughts.

He kept his back to her as he pulled on his pants and shirt. Not that she could see in the dark any more than he could. But all things considered, it just seemed like the right thing to do.

"I really am sorry." He knew his apologies weren't nearly adequate enough for the circumstances, but then he wasn't sure anything he could say or do would make the situation any less humiliating for either of them. "I swear to God, I thought you were Lori."

"I'm her…sister," the woman said, sounding like she might be recovering her ability to speak in a complete sentence.

He knew Lori had a sister, but since their relationship was mostly physical, he and Lori hadn't delved too deeply into the details of each other's lives. And if she had mentioned her sister by name, he'd be damned if he could think of it now.

"I'd give anything if this hadn't—"

"Please, don't," she said, cutting him off. "Just leave…Josh."

He hesitated, then, deciding that it was probably

the best—the only—thing he could do, he walked to the front door and let himself out of the apartment. He had no sooner pulled the door shut than he heard her set the dead bolt and slide the chain into place.

His heart stalled for a moment, then began to beat double time. He had been just drunk enough and she apparently had been sleepy enough for both of them to forget the use of a condom. It was something he had never forgotten before and he couldn't believe that he'd done so this time.

Completely sober now, he shook his head as he walked the short distance to his Mercedes still sitting in the restaurant's parking lot. He was going to drive home and when he woke up in the morning, he hoped to discover that he'd dreamed the entire incident.

But as he got into the car and started the engine, he knew as surely as the sun rose in the east each morning that wasn't going to be the case. Nothing was going to change the fact that he had done the unthinkable. He had made love to his girlfriend's sister—the most exciting, responsive woman he had ever met. And what was even worse, he had no clue what she looked like and didn't even know her name.

One

Three years later

Standing in the hallway outside the meeting rooms at the Texas Cattleman's Club, Kiley Roberts sighed heavily. If she hadn't had enough problems dealing with the vandalism of the club's new day care center a few months ago, now she was about to face the funding committee to ask for an increase in funds to run it. Unfortunately, from everything she had heard, she was facing an uphill battle. Several of the committeemen had been extremely vocal about not seeing the need to provide child care for club members, and among them was the chairman of the funding committee, Josh Gordon.

They had never been formally introduced and she didn't even know if he knew who she was. But she knew him and just the thought of having to deal with the man made her cringe with embarrassment.

Every detail of what happened that night three years ago had played through her mind since discovering that Josh was a member of the club. But when she learned he was chairman of the funding committee— the very committee that controlled the money to run the day care center—she felt as if she'd been kicked in the stomach. Being the center's director, she had to go to the committee for approval on everything outside of the budget they had set for it. That meant she would frequently have to deal with him.

She took a deep fortifying breath. How could fate be so cruel?

If she hadn't been half-asleep and wanting so badly to believe that Mark—her then-boyfriend and now ex-husband—had followed her to her sister's apartment to apologize for the argument they'd had, the incident three years ago would have never taken place. She would have realized right away that Josh wasn't Mark and stopped him before things went too far.

Kiley shook her head at her own foolishness. She should have known when Josh kissed her with such passion that the man in bed with her wasn't Mark. The only thing Mark had ever been passionate about was himself.

Sighing, she straightened her shoulders. There was nothing she could do about it now, and there was no sense in dwelling on something she couldn't change. She just wished anyone other than Josh Gordon was heading up the funding committee. Aside from the humiliating incident, he had broken her sister's heart when he abruptly ended things between them a month or so after that fateful night, and Kiley simply didn't trust him.

When the door to the meeting room opened, interrupting her tumultuous thoughts, a man she assumed to be one of the members motioned toward her. "Ms. Roberts, the committee is ready to hear from you now."

Nodding, Kiley took a deep breath and forced her feet to move forward when what she really wanted to do was turn around and head in the opposite direction. "Thank you."

As she walked toward the long table at the head of the room where Josh sat with three men and a woman, she focused on them instead of Josh. The only two she recognized were Beau Hacket and Paul Windsor. Great. They seemed to be the unofficial leaders of those opposed to the day care center and it was just her luck that they both happened to be on the funding committee. Kiley's only hope was to appeal to the lone female member and the man sitting next to her.

"Good afternoon," she said, forcing herself to give them all a cheerful smile when she was feeling anything but optimistic.

"What can we do for you today…" Josh glanced at the papers on the table in front of him as if checking for her name "…Ms. Roberts?"

When their gazes finally met, she felt a little better. She had been hired by the club's personnel director and had managed to avoid coming face-to-face with Josh in the short time she had been working at the Texas Cattleman's Club. But now, she realized her nervousness had been unfounded. Apparently Lori had never mentioned her by name and thanks to the blackout curtains her sister preferred, neither of them had been able to see the other that night. Deciding he was either a good enough actor to deserve an Academy Award or he had no idea who she was, her confidence returned.

"As the director, I'm here to ask the committee to consider appropriating additional funds for the day care center," she stated, surprised her voice sounded strong and steady in spite of her earlier case of jangled nerves.

"What for?" Beau Hacket demanded. "We've already budgeted more than is necessary to babysit a bunch of little kids."

"I can't believe you just said that," the middle-aged woman seated to Josh's right said, glaring at Beau.

Kiley watched Josh give the man a disapproving glare before he turned his attention back to her. "What do you think you need the additional funds for, Ms. Roberts?"

"The club members' response to the day care center has been so positive, we have more children than we first anticipated," she answered, already knowing from the negative expression on his face how Beau Hacket would be voting on the matter.

"All you're doing is watching a handful of little kids for a couple of hours," Beau spoke up. "I don't see where you need more money for that. Sit them down with a crayon and a piece of paper and they'll be happy."

"Beau."

There was a warning in Josh's tone, but Kiley knew it was more a rule of order than any kind of support for her. Josh Gordon had been almost as vocal in his objections to the day care center as Beau Hacket and Paul Windsor had. Since the club started admitting female members a few years ago, the TCC had experienced quite a few growing pains as it made changes to accommodate the needs of women in its ranks, the most recent change being the addition of the day care center.

Focusing her attention on the others seated at the conference table and off the committee chairman, she decided it was time to set them straight. "I think some of you have a few misconceptions about the day care center. Yes, we do provide a safe environment for the members to leave their children while they attend meetings or events at the clubhouse, but we're more than just a babysitting service. Some of the members depend on us for early childhood education, as well."

"My granddaughter is one of your students and in the short time she's been attending, we've all been amazed at how much she's learned," the woman seated beside Josh said, smiling.

"Why can't they teach their own kids how to finger-paint at home?" Beau demanded, his disapproval evident in the tone of his voice as he glared at her.

"I'm trained in early childhood education," Kiley explained, hoping to convince the man of the importance of day care, but knowing she probably wouldn't. "The center's programs are age appropriate and structured so that the children are engaged in learning activities for their level of development." When the committee members frowned in obvious confusion, she rushed on to keep one of them from cutting her off. "For example, the toddlers learn how to interact and share with other children, as well as begin to develop friendships and basic social skills. The preschool class learns to recognize and print the letters of the alphabet, as well as their names. And in addition to teaching them how to count, my assistant and I play learning games with both groups designed to pique their interest in things like science and nature." She shook her head. "The list is endless and I could stay here all day outlining the importance of early child-hood education and the benefits to a child."

When Kiley stopped to take a breath, the woman on the committee nodded. "My granddaughter has not only learned a lot, she's conquered some of her shyness and has become more outgoing, as well."

Appreciative of the woman's support, Kiley smiled. At least she had one advocate on the committee.

Josh glanced down at the papers on the table in front of him. "You're not asking for more space, just additional money for the center?"

"No, the size of the room isn't a problem. We have enough room for the children we have now, as well as many more." She could tell he wasn't paying much at-tention to what she had to say and would probably like to deny her outright. But protocol called for the com-mittee to hear her out, discuss her request, then take a vote on the issue. "All I'm asking for is additional money for the day-to-day operation of the center."

"Since you don't have utilities or rent to worry about, what specifically would the funds be used for?" Paul Windsor asked, giving her a charming smile. A ladies' man if there ever was one, the older gentleman's flirtatious smile didn't fool Kiley one bit. He was just as opposed to the day care center as Beau Hacket.

"Some of the children are with us for the entire day, instead of a half day or just a few hours, Mr. Windsor," she answered, relieved she wasn't having to focus on Josh, even though she didn't like Paul Windsor. "We need the extra money for the materials for their activities, as well as the additional lunches and snacks. We also need to hire an extra worker for the infants we occasionally have when their mothers have a tennis match or engage in some of the other activities here at the clubhouse."

"We wouldn't have this problem if we hadn't let women into the club," Beau muttered as he sat back in his chair to glare at her.

"What was that, Beau?" the woman demanded, looking as if she was ready to do battle.

Beau shook his head as he belligerently folded his arms across his barrel chest. "I didn't say a damned thing, Nadine."

Kiley wasn't the least bit surprised at the man's comment or the woman's reaction. Beau Hacket was one of the men still resentful of women being permitted membership into the prestigious club, and the female members had quickly learned to stand up to the "good old boy network" and demand the respect they deserved.

"Is there anything else you'd like to add?" Josh asked, clearly ready to dismiss her and move on to the discussion phase.

"No, I believe I've adequately outlined the purpose of the day care center and the reasons we need the extra funds," she said, knowing in her heart that her plea had fallen on deaf ears—at least where the male members of the committee were concerned.

He nodded. "I think we have more than enough information to consider your request. Thank you for your time and detailed explanation, Ms. Roberts."

Looking up at her, he smiled and Kiley felt as if

the floor moved beneath her feet. His bright blue eyes and engaging smile sent a shiver of awareness coursing from the top of her head to the soles of her feet and, as much as she would have liked to forget, she couldn't stop thinking about what happened that night three years ago.

"I'll drop by the center later this afternoon to let you know the outcome of our vote," Josh finished, oblivious to her reaction.

Feeling as if having to listen to her had been an inconvenience for them, Kiley nodded and walked from the meeting room. There was nothing left for her to do now but await the committee's decision. She wished she felt more positive about the results of their vote. Unfortunately, with three of the center's biggest opponents on the committee, a favorable outcome was highly unlikely.

But as much as she feared hearing their decision, Kiley dreaded having to see Josh again even more. Why couldn't he send one of the other members to let her know what had been decided? Didn't she already have enough on her plate without having to worry about seeing him again?

She had a two-year-old daughter to care for and a house that seemed to be in constant need of one repair or another, and, if the additional money for the day care didn't come through, the center might have to close due to a clause in the club's amended bylaws assuring that no member's child would be turned away, and she would be out of a job. And even if he didn't know who she was, she certainly didn't need the added stress of being reminded of the most embarrassing incident of her entire life.

* * *

As Josh walked down the hall toward the day care center, he couldn't for the life of him figure out why he felt as though he knew Kiley Roberts. He didn't think they had met before she walked into the meeting room earlier in the afternoon. If they had, he knew for certain he would have remembered her. A woman that attractive would be damned near impossible to forget.

Normally he preferred his women tall, willowy and with an air of mystery about them. But Kiley made petite and curvy look good—real good. With her chin-length, dark blond hair and the prettiest brown eyes he had ever seen, she looked soft, sexy and very approachable.

He frowned as he tried to remember if he'd even seen her before this afternoon. She might have been at Beau Hacket's barbecue a few months back. It seemed that Hacket had invited the entire membership of the Texas Cattleman's Club, as well as most of the residents of Royal. Or more likely he'd seen her somewhere around the clubhouse, maybe in the restaurant or the bar. But he couldn't shake the feeling that there was more to it than that.

When he reached the door to the old billiard room—now renovated to house the day care center—he shrugged. It really didn't matter. Once he gave her the news that she wouldn't be getting any more money from the club, he would go straight to the top of her Grinch list and that would be the end of that.

Looking through the window in the door, he noticed that the room looked much nicer now than it had a couple of months ago when vandals broke in and tore up the place. They still hadn't caught who was behind the destruction or their motive for doing it, but Josh felt sure the culprits would eventually be caught and dealt with accordingly. Royal, Texas, wasn't that big of a town, and many of its residents were members of the TCC. It was just a matter of time before someone remembered seeing or hearing something that would lead the authorities to make an arrest.

He would hate to be in the vandals' shoes when that happened, he thought as he opened the day care center's door. Whether the place was wanted by all of the members or not, nobody came in and destroyed any part of their clubhouse without the entire membership taking great exception to it.

"I'll be right with you, Mr. Gordon," Kiley said from across the room.

"Take your time," he said, looking around. Several children sat in pint-size chairs at tables that were just as small. He couldn't imagine ever being little enough to fit into furniture that size.

As he watched, Russ and Winnie Bartlett's youngest little girl got out of her chair and walked over to hold up a paper with crayon scribbles for Kiley's inspection. She acted as if the kid had just drawn the *Mona Lisa,* causing the toddler to beam with pride.

Josh had never taken much to little kids. For one thing, he had never been around them and didn't have a clue how to relate to them. But he found himself smiling as he watched Kiley talk to the child as she pinned the drawing to a bulletin board. Only a coldhearted bastard would ignore the fact that she had just made the little girl's day.

"Carrie, could you take over for me for a few minutes?" she asked a young woman Josh assumed to be the day care worker Kiley had hired not long after the center opened. When the woman nodded, Kiley walked over to him and motioned toward a door on the far side of the room. "Why don't we go into my office? Otherwise, I can't guarantee we won't be interrupted."

As he followed her to her office, he found himself fascinated by the slight sway of her hips. He had to force himself to keep his eyes trained on her slender shoulders. But that only drew his attention to the exposed skin between the collar of her red sweater and the bottom of her short blond hair—a spot that looked extremely kissable.

His heart thumped hard against his rib cage and heat began to fill his lower belly. What the hell was wrong with him? Had it been that long since he and his last girlfriend parted ways?

"Please have a seat, Mr. Gordon," Kiley said, walking behind the small desk to sit down in an old wooden chair.

He recognized both the desk and the chair as having been in the storage room for as long as he had been a member of the club and probably for decades before that. If circumstances had been different, he might have felt guilty about the funding committee insisting her office be furnished with the club's castoffs. But considering none of the members on the panel, with maybe the exception of Nadine Capshaw, expected the center to remain open past spring, it had been decided that the used furniture would be good enough.

"Call me Josh," he said, sitting in a metal folding chair across the desk from her.

"I assume you've come to tell me the funding committee's decision on my request…Josh?" she asked, sounding as if she already knew the outcome of the vote.

There was something about the sound of her voice saying his name that caused him to frown. "Before we get into the committee's decision, could I ask you something?"

"I…uh, suppose so." He could tell by the hesitation in her voice and her wary expression that she didn't trust him.

"Do we know each other?" he asked, realizing immediately from the slight widening of her expressive brown eyes that they did.

"No," she said a little too quickly.

"Are you sure?" he pressed, determined to find out what she knew that he didn't.

"Well, we…um, don't know each other formally," she said, suddenly taking great interest in her tightly clasped hands resting on top of the desk.

She was hiding something, and he intended to find out what it was. "So we have met?" he continued.

"In a way…I guess you could say that." Her knuckles had turned white from her tight grip and he knew whatever she hid was extremely stressful for her. "It was quite by accident."

Every hair follicle on his head felt as if it stood straight up, and he suddenly wasn't so sure he wanted to know what she obviously didn't want to tell him. "Where would that have been?" he heard himself ask in spite of his reservations.

Getting up, she closed her office door, then slowly lowered herself into the chair when she returned to the desk. "You used to date my sister."

A cold, clammy feeling snaked its way up his spine. "I did?"

When she finally raised her head to meet his gaze head-on, a knot the size of his fist began to twist his gut. "I'm Lori Miller's sister. Her *only* sister."

Josh opened his mouth, then snapped it shut. For the first time in his adult life, he couldn't think of a thing to say. But his unusual reaction to her suddenly started to make sense. From the moment she'd walked into the meeting room to plead her case to the funding committee, he had been fighting to keep his libido under control. Now he knew why. He might not have realized who she was, but apparently his body had. The chemistry between them that night three years ago had been undeniable and it appeared that it was just as powerful now. Unless he missed his guess, her nervousness had just as much to do with the magnetic pull between them as it did with her reluctance to admit what had taken place.

As he stared at her, it occurred to him why Kiley seemed familiar to him. Although it had been too dark to tell what she looked like that night, he could see the resemblance between her and her sister now. Kiley had the same extraordinary brown eyes and flawless alabaster skin that Lori had. But that seemed to be where the similarities between the two women ended. While Lori was considerably taller and had auburn hair, Kiley was shorter and had dark blond hair that looked so silky it practically begged a man to tangle his fingers in it as he made love to her. When his lower body began to tighten, he swallowed hard and tried to think of something—anything—to get his mind back on track.

"Your last name is different," he stated the obvious.

She straightened her shoulders and took a deep breath. "I was married briefly."

"But not anymore?" he couldn't stop himself from asking.

"No."

He swallowed hard as a thought suddenly occurred to him. "You weren't married—"

"No. Not then."

Relieved that he hadn't crossed that particular line, Josh released the breath he hadn't been aware of holding. "That's good."

"Look, I'm not any happier than you are about having to work with you on the day care center's funding," she said, her cheeks coloring a pretty pink. "But this isn't the time or the place to get into what happened that night. I think it would be for the best if we forgot the incident ever happened and concentrate on my request for the day care center and the committee's decision not to give me the extra money I need to keep it running."

He knew she was right. A day care center full of little kids certainly wasn't the place to talk over his mistakenly making love to her. And she had a valid point about forgetting that night. It would definitely be the prudent thing to do. But some perverse part of him resented her wanting to dismiss what had arguably been the most exciting night of his life. He'd never been with a woman, either before or since, as responsive and passionate as Kiley had been.

"I agree," he finally said. "We can take a trip down memory lane another time." He could tell his choice of words and the fact that he thought they should revisit the past wasn't what she wanted to hear.

She folded her arms beneath her breasts, causing his mouth to go dry. "Mr. Gordon—"

"I prefer you call me Josh," he reminded her.

"Josh, I think you'd better—"

"I have good news and bad news," he said, thinking quickly. If her body language was any indication, she was about two seconds away from throwing him out of her office.

Whether it was due to the lingering guilt he still harbored over his part in the incident or the distrust he detected in her big brown eyes, he wasn't sure. But he suddenly felt the need to prove to her that she had the wrong opinion of him.

"I'm going to give you a month's worth of the funding you requested in order for you to convince me that the day care center is worthwhile and a needed addition to the services the club provides to the TCC membership," he stated, before she could interrupt.

She frowned. "That isn't what the committee decided, is it?"

"Not exactly," he said honestly. "The committee voted four to one to deny you the extra money. But after seeing the way you were with the Bartletts' little girl, you've got my attention. I'll be checking in periodically to see for myself that the money was needed and put to good use."

If anything, she looked even more skeptical. "What happens at the end of that time?"

"If I determine that you do need the additional funding, at our meeting just before Christmas I'll give my personal recommendation to the committee that we add the amount you asked for to your yearly bud-get," he finished.

"If my request was turned down, where is this money going to come from?" she asked, looking more suspicious by the second.

"You let me worry about that," he said, rising to his feet. "I'll see that the appropriate amount is added to the day care's account as of this afternoon. It should be accessible for whatever you need by tomorrow morn-ing."

Before she could question him further, he opened her office door and left to go to the TCC's main office to make arrangements for the funding to be put into the day care's account. He was going to be taking the money out of his own pocket to subsidize the center for the next month, but it would be worth it. For one thing, he wanted to prove to her that he wasn't the ne-farious SOB she apparently thought him to be. And for another, it was the only thing he could think of that might come close to atoning for his role in what hap-pened three years ago.

Two

Kiley spent most of the next day jumping every time the door to the day care center opened. True to his word, Josh had added money to the center's account and she did appreciate that. But it was his promised visits to observe how she ran things and to see what the funds were being used for that had her nerves stretched to the breaking point. She didn't want to see him again or have to jump through hoops to get the money the center needed. Besides, every time she looked into his blue eyes, it reminded her that they shared a very intimate secret—one that, try as she might, she couldn't forget.

"The children have put away the toys and I've finished reading them a story. Would you like for me to take them outside to the play area for a bit before we start practicing their songs?" Carrie Kramer asked, walking over to where Kiley had finished putting stars by the names of the children who had remembered to wash their hands before their afternoon snack.

"That would be great." Kiley smiled at the young woman she'd hired to be her assistant after meeting her at the Royal Diner. "While they expend some of their excess energy outside, I'll get things ready for us to practice their songs before they go home."

As she watched Carrie help the children get their coats on and form a single line by the exit to the play yard, Kiley turned to go into her office for the things they would be using for the holiday program they were putting on for the parents the week before Christmas. Gathering the props, she decided she would have to make two trips as she turned to retrace her steps back into the main room. Distracted as she tried to remember everything they would need, she ran headlong into Josh standing just inside the doorway to her office.

"Oh, my dear heavens!" The giant jingle bells in the box she carried jangled loudly as she struggled to hang on to it.

Placing his hands on her shoulders to steady her, he frowned. "I didn't mean to frighten you. I called your name when I found the other room empty."

The warmth of his hands seemed to burn through her pink silk blouse. Kiley quickly took a step back. "I must not have heard it over the sound of these bells."

"Let me help you with these," he said, taking the box from her. "Where are the kids?"

"My assistant took them outside for playtime before we start practicing for their Christmas program," she said, picking up her CD player and several large plastic candy canes.

Their arms brushed as she walked past him, and an awareness she hadn't felt in a very long time caused her heart to skip several beats. She did her best to ignore it.

"I intended to stop by earlier in the day, but I got tied up at one of our construction sites and it took longer than I anticipated," he said, following her over to the brightly colored carpet where the children gathered for story time. "I wasn't sure anyone would still be here. When do the kids go home?"

"Normally, all of the children get picked up by five-thirty," she answered, setting the candy canes and the CD player on a small table. "But Gil Addison sometimes gets detained by club business and runs a few minutes late picking up his son, Cade." A single father, the current president of the TCC had been one of the first to enroll his four-year-old son in the preschool class. Unlike the members of the funding committee, Gil seemed extremely enthusiastic about having the center at the clubhouse. "No matter what time it is, I stay until every child is safely in the care of their parents or someone they've designated to pick up the child."

"So this isn't just a nine-to-five job, then?" he asked, placing the box on the carpet.

"Not hardly." Shaking her head, she removed a disc from its case to put in the player. "I have to be here at seven each morning to get things ready for the children's arrival."

"When is that?" he asked, his brow furrowing.

"A couple of them get here a few minutes after I do, but they're all here between eight and eight-thirty," she said, wondering why he was so interested in the hours the day care center operated. "Why do you ask?"

He ran his hand through his short, light brown hair. "I realize you're working on contract with the club and aren't paid overtime, no matter how many hours you work, but doesn't that make for a pretty long day?"

She couldn't help but smile. Being able to be with her daughter while she did her job was well worth any extra time she had to put in at the center. "I don't mind. This is my dream job."

"I guess if that's what makes you happy," he said, looking as if he couldn't understand anyone feeling that way about working those kinds of hours with a group of small children.

When the children began filing into the room from outside, Kiley breathed a sigh of relief. It wasn't that she was afraid of Josh. But being alone with him made her feel jumpy and she welcomed the distraction of a roomful of toddlers and preschoolers. She wasn't at all happy about the effect he had on her and refused to think about why he made her feel that way. She was almost certain she wouldn't like the answer.

"After you've hung up your coats, I want you all to come over to the carpet and sit down, please," she announced to the children. "We're going to practice our songs for your Christmas program before you go home this afternoon."

Her daughter ran over to wrap her arms around one of Kiley's legs, then looked up at her and giggled. "Me sing."

"That's right, Emmie," Kiley said, stroking her daughter's dark blond hair as she smiled down at the only good to come out of her brief marriage. "Can you go over and sit with Elaina and Bobby so we can get started, please?"

Emmie nodded, then hurried over to join her two friends where they sat with the rest of the toddlers.

"Miss Kiley, Jimmy Joe Harper pulled my hair," Sarah Bartlett accused, glaring at the little boy seated beside her.

"Jimmy Joe, did you pull Sarah's hair again?" Even before he nodded, one look at the impish grin on the child's face told Kiley that he had. "I'm sorry, but I told you that if you pulled Sarah's pigtails again you'd have to sit in the 'time out' corner for five minutes."

Without further instruction, the child obediently got to his feet and walked over to sit in a chair by himself in the far corner of the room. When she noticed Josh glancing from her to Jimmy Joe in the "time out" corner, Kiley raised an eyebrow. "Is there something wrong?"

"You didn't even have to tell him to go over there," he said, sounding as if he couldn't quite believe a child would willingly accept his punishment. "And he didn't protest at all."

"Jimmy Joe is no stranger to the 'time out' corner," Kiley answered, smiling fondly at the adorable red-haired little boy. "He loves aggravating Sarah."

Josh looked confused. "Why?"

"Because he likes her." Kiley turned to her assistant. "Could you please pass out the bells and candy canes, Carrie?"

"I see," Josh said as a slow grin curved the corners of his mouth. "In other words, he's teasing her to keep her attention focused on him."

"Something...like that," Kiley said, her breath

catching at how handsome Josh looked when he smiled.

As her assistant finished handing each child an oversize bell or a giant plastic candy cane, Kiley queued up the music on her CD player and purposely avoided looking at Josh. He made her nervous and she wished he would leave. But it appeared as if he intended to stay for a while.

Deciding that as long as he was there, he might as well participate, she picked up one of the bells and shoved it into his hand. "I assume you know the words to 'Jingle Bells'?"

He looked surprised, then determined as he shook his head. "Yes, I'm familiar with the song, but I'm afraid I can't stay. I promised a friend I would stop by his place this afternoon and I'm already running late."

"That's a shame," she lied. She had accomplished what she set out to do. He was going to leave. She couldn't help but smile. "Maybe another time."

"Yeah, maybe," he said, sounding doubtful. He reached out and, taking her hand in his, placed the bell in the center of her palm, then gently folded her fingers around it with his other hand. "Will you be free tomorrow evening?"

Startled by his unexpected question and the warmth of his hands holding hers, she stared at him a moment before she managed to find her voice. "Wh-why?"

"I'd like to discuss a couple of things with you," he said evasively. He gave her a smile that made her insides flutter. "Unfortunately, I don't have time to talk to you about it now. I'll come by here around five-thirty on Friday evening and we'll have dinner in the club's restaurant. They have an excellent menu and we'll be able to talk without interruption."

Kiley opened her mouth to refuse, but when he tenderly caressed her hand with his, she forgot anything she was about to say. As she watched him walk across the room to the door, she shook her head in an effort to regain her equilibrium.

What was Josh up to? And what did he think they needed to discuss? She had been quite clear when she spoke to the funding committee about the use of the extra money for the day care center. Surely he couldn't want to talk about what happened that night....

"Miss Kiley, can I go back to the carpet now?" Jimmy Joe asked from the "time out" corner.

"'May I go back to the carpet,'" Kiley automatically corrected.

"May I?" the little boy asked, flashing his charming grin.

"Yes, you may," she said, deciding that she could give more thought to Josh and his dinner invitation after the children had gone home for the day.

Kiley went through the motions of rehearsing the Christmas show the children would put on for their parents in a few weeks. But her mind kept straying back to Josh and his ridiculous invitation. Even if she were willing to go to dinner with him—which she wasn't—she didn't think he would be all that enthusiastic about dining with a two-year-old.

It wasn't that Emmie wasn't well-behaved. She was. But by the end of the day, she was tired and wanted nothing more than dinner, a bath and to go to bed. Besides, there was absolutely nothing Kiley felt the need to discuss with Josh. Now or in the foreseeable future.

* * *

As Josh drove his Mercedes through the gates of Pine Valley, the exclusive golf course community where several of the TCC members had built mansions, he couldn't help but wonder what he'd been thinking when he asked Kiley to dinner. Why couldn't he just drop what had happened that night three years ago?

He knew that would be the smartest thing to do and what Kiley wanted. But for reasons he didn't want to delve into, some perverse part of him wanted her to admit that, although the circumstances that brought them together that night might have been an unfortunate accident, their lovemaking had been nothing short of amazing.

"You've lost your mind, Gordon," he muttered as he steered his car onto Alex Santiago's private drive.

Doing his best to forget the matter, he parked in front of the palatial home, got out of the car and climbed the steps to the front door. Before he could ring the doorbell, the door opened.

"Hello, Señor Gordon," a round-faced older woman with kind brown eyes said, stepping back for Josh to enter. "Señor Alex is in the sunroom."

"How's he feeling today, Maria?" Josh asked as the housekeeper whom Alex's fiancée, Cara Windsor, had recently hired led the way toward the back of the elegant home.

Maria stopped, then, turning to face him, gave Josh a worried look. "Señor Alex still has headaches and can't remember anything before he was found."

"I'm sure it's just a matter of time before he recovers his memory." Josh wasn't entirely sure who he was trying to reassure—the housekeeper or himself.

Alex had been missing for several months before being found, suffering a head injury, in the back of a truck with a group of migrant farm workers smuggled across the border from Mexico. No one seemed to know how he wound up across the border or how he got into the back of the truck with the workers, and he couldn't tell the authorities anything. There was strong evidence that he had been beaten several times and one theory was that he had been kidnapped. But no matter what had happened, Alex still had amnesia. It had only been recently that he'd been released from Royal Memorial Hospital. With Cara's encouragement, Alex's friends from the TCC had been taking turns dropping by to check on his progress. No one had said as much, but Josh knew they all hoped to help him recover his memory so they could find whoever had done this to him.

"How are you feeling today, Alex?" he asked, walking into the sunroom where his friend sat reading a book.

Alex smiled and slowly rose to his feet to extend his hand. "Josh, isn't it?"

Nodding, Josh shook Alex's hand. The man's grip was firm and Josh took that as a good sign that his friend was regaining some of his strength. But he was still cautious about making sure he called his friends by the correct name, which indicated his memory wasn't much better.

"I wanted to stop by and let you know that we're all hoping to see you and Cara at the Christmas Ball." Before his disappearance in the summer, Alex had been on the planning committee for the annual holiday gala. Josh hoped that referring to the event might spark a memory.

"Yes, Cara and I discussed it and we're hoping that being at the Texas Cattleman's Club with all of my acquaintances will help me remember something," Alex answered. He sighed heavily. "It's damned irritating not being able to remember anything about my life before waking up in the back of that truck."

"I'm sure there will be a break in the case soon," Josh said, hoping he was right. "The Royal Police Department's detective unit is one of the best in the entire state and they're letting Britt Collins, the state investigator, take the lead. With her FBI training and specialty in kidnapping cases, they'll have whoever did this to you behind bars in no time."

"I was told this morning they intend to send my picture to the national television networks in an attempt to find anyone who might have seen who I was with while I was missing. It might also help locate any family I have," Alex added. "Apparently none of them live close by, because there haven't been any family members respond to the local news reports about me."

Josh smiled. "I'm sure the news of all this going national will help to escalate the investigation."

As they continued to discuss Alex's frustration with his lack of memory and the possibility of the police turning up something that would give them a clue who had beaten him, Josh's mind kept straying back to Kiley and his invitation to dinner the following evening. It suddenly occurred to him that she hadn't said no.

Of course, she hadn't exactly accepted his invitation either. But he decided not to give that a second thought. As far as he was concerned they were having dinner tomorrow evening and he fully intended to discuss that night three years ago. He needed for her to understand that he wasn't in the habit of making love to a woman he didn't know, then leaving her like some kind of thief in the night. He also wanted her to admit that she had played a part in the incident when she had been so receptive to him. Then, as far as he was concerned, the matter would be closed for good.

Satisfied that he had a viable plan, he filled Alex in on things that were going on at the clubhouse. "The day care center is open and has quite a few kids attending."

"I am sure the female members are happy about that," Alex said, smiling. "But Cara tells me her father and a few others are less supportive."

Josh nodded. "I wasn't entirely sure it's needed, but after the director's request for more money to operate the center I'm taking the time to learn more about it before I make up my mind."

"It is always good to keep an open mind and get the facts before one passes judgment," Alex said, nodding.

As Josh listened to Alex, he appreciated the wisdom in his friend's quietly spoken observation. "Thanks for the advice. I'll be sure to do just that." Rising to leave, he shook Alex's hand. "You know if you need anything, all you have to do is give me a call."

"I appreciate that, Josh," Alex said, following him to the front door. "I will certainly keep that in mind."

As Josh descended the front steps, he noticed a car coming up the long drive. When it pulled to a stop behind his and the driver got out, he recognized Alex's former housekeeper, Mia Hughes.

She waved. "Hi, Josh. How is Alex doing today?"

"He's frustrated with his lack of memory, but that's to be expected." He smiled. "I hear that congratulations are in order."

The pretty young woman beamed. "You heard about my engagement to Dave Firestone?"

"Yes." He laughed. "News like that travels through the TCC like a flash fire through a wood pile."

She laughed. "Thank you, Josh. I've never been happier."

"If the smile on Firestone's face these days is any indication, I'd say he's just as happy," Josh said.

"It was nice seeing you again, Josh," Mia said as she started up the steps to the front door.

Josh nodded. "I'll see you in a few weeks at the Christmas Ball."

Getting into the car, he drove away from the Santiago mansion feeling pretty good about the day. He had successfully straightened out a problem with the work crew on one of the Gordon Construction job sites, had a nice visit with his friend and had set up dinner with Kiley Roberts for tomorrow evening.

"A very good day," he said aloud as he drove across town to his ranch just outside Royal.

The next afternoon, Kiley tried to remain focused and not think about Josh stopping by, expecting her to go to dinner with him. But try as she might, every time the door opened, she looked up expectantly. So far, it had been parents arriving to pick up their children, but she knew it was just a matter of time before she looked up to find Josh entering the day care center.

Of course, she had no intention of going anywhere

with him. But how could she anticipate and dread him stopping by all at the same time?

"Kiley, would you mind if I leave now?" Carrie asked, looking hopeful. "There are only two more children to be picked up by their parents and I have an appointment at the hair salon in fifteen minutes."

"Do you have a date with Ron tonight?" Kiley asked. From the time the young woman started working for her, Carrie had chattered nonstop about her boyfriend and Kiley expected any day to hear that they had become engaged.

Her assistant nodded. "He's taking me out to dinner and then we're going to see the new Channing Tatum movie."

"You can only leave early on one condition."

"What's that?" her assistant asked cautiously.

Kiley grinned. "You have to tell me all about the movie and how many times Channing takes his shirt off."

Carrie laughed as she grabbed her coat and purse from the closet by the door. "I can do that."

"Have a nice evening, and I'll see you tomorrow morning, Carrie."

As her assistant rushed out the door to get her hair done for her date, Kiley's heart skipped a beat when Josh walked in. Dressed in a black suit, pale blue shirt and navy tie, he looked more handsome than any man had the right to look outside the pages of *GQ*.

"Instead of making a reservation for us in the restaurant here at the club, I thought we might try that new place on the west side of town," Josh said, flashing her a smile that sent goose bumps shimmering up her arms. "Have all of the kids gone home?"

"Not yet." She collected the Santa Claus faces made of construction paper and cotton balls that the preschool class had made during their craft time. "But I'm afraid I won't be able to…" She let her voice trail off when Russ and Winnie Bartlett entered the day care center to pick up their two little girls.

While Josh shook hands with Russ and talked about the upcoming meeting of the general membership, Kiley and Winnie chatted about the children's holiday program.

"It's all Sarah can talk about," Winnie said, smiling at her little girl. As she helped her youngest daughter into her jacket, she laughed and smoothed her toddler's straight dark hair. "And Elaina tells me she's going to be one of the 'kidney' canes."

Grinning, Kiley nodded. "She calls them 'kidney' canes and Emmie calls them 'kitty' canes."

"Isn't it fun deciphering what a two-year-old means as they learn new words?" Winnie asked.

"Oh, yes." When Emmie toddled over to give Elaina a goodbye hug, Kiley smiled fondly at her beautiful little girl. "At times it feels like they speak a foreign language."

After the Bartletts bid them a good evening, Kiley and Emmie were left alone with Josh. Turning toward her office to retrieve her purse, Kiley heard Emmie start chattering about her toy ponies. Glancing over her shoulder, she almost laughed out loud at Josh's perplexed expression.

"Me pony," Emmie said, reaching up to wrap her little hand around one of Josh's fingers to tug him in the direction of the play area.

"What does she want?" Josh asked, sounding a little

alarmed. He might have been bewildered about what Emmie wanted, but to his credit, he followed her over to the toy box on the other side of the room.

"She wants to show you her favorite toys," Kiley said, quickly grabbing her things and switching off the office light.

"That's nice." Josh smiled when Emmie held up a purple pony with a flowing white mane and tail. "How much longer before one of her parents arrives to get her?"

"Emmie goes home with me," Kiley said, taking their coats from the closet. "She's my daughter."

"I didn't realize you had a child," he said, glancing down at Emmie digging through the toys to find more ponies.

When he looked back at her, Kiley could tell by his expression that Josh realized her going to dinner with him wasn't going to happen. But as they continued to stare at each other, a mischievous spark lit his brilliant blue eyes.

"So you like ponies and horses, Emmie?" he asked.

Emmie vigorously nodded her little blond head. "Yes."

Squatting down to her level, he handed the toy pony back to her. "I like horses, too. I have several of them at my ranch."

Emmie's little face lit up. "Me wanna see."

"I think that can be arranged," Josh said, giving Kiley a triumphant grin.

Kiley didn't like the idea in the least. "I don't think that would be—"

"Why don't you ask your mother to bring you over to my ranch on Saturday afternoon so I can show you my horses?" he asked before Kiley could stop him from making the offer.

"Pease, Mommy?" Emmie asked, skipping over to her. "Pease. Wanna see ponies. Wanna see ponies."

Kiley was fit to be tied. Josh had deliberately manipulated the situation and now her daughter looked so hopeful, she hated to refuse. But on the other hand, she didn't want to spend more time with Josh than she had to. Nor was she overly happy about his taking control of the situation.

"Is this retaliation for not going to dinner with you?" she asked, delaying her answer. A thought suddenly occurred to her. "You aren't going to let this influence your decision about the funding for the day care center, are you?"

"Not at all." A frown creased his forehead as he rose to his full height and walked over to her and Emmie. "I just thought your little girl might like to see a real horse."

"You knew she would," Kiley accused.

"Not really," Josh said, rocking back on his heels. "I don't know enough about little kids to know whether she would or not."

She wasn't buying his innocent expression for a minute. "This is punishment for not going to dinner with you and we both know it."

"Oh, I wouldn't go so far as to call it that." Standing closer than she was comfortable with, he leaned over to whisper, "And no. I won't let this influence my recommendation to the funding committee. Although you could have told me sooner that dinner wasn't really an option."

"You didn't give me a chance yesterday afternoon,"

she said defensively. "And you didn't come by the center earlier for me to tell you."

"We both know you could have called my office or left a message for me here at the clubhouse," he reminded, his voice so intimate it sent a tiny shiver of awareness straight up her spine. "So what do you say?" he asked, smiling. "You just said yourself that Emmie would like seeing the horses."

The woodsy scent of his cologne and the fact that he stood so close were playing havoc with her equilibrium. Taking a step away from him, she looked down at Emmie. Her daughter looked so excited and happy, how could Kiley possibly disappoint her?

"Oh, all right," she finally conceded. "But we'll only stop by for a few minutes."

"Good." Josh gave her directions to his ranch just outside of town. "I'll expect you and Emmie around one." Bending down, he smiled at her daughter. "I'll see you in a few days, Emmie." Straightening, he lightly touched her cheek with his index finger. "Have a nice evening, Kiley."

As she watched him stroll to the door, a shiver coursed through her at his light touch and the sound of his rich baritone saying her name. She shook her head to clear it.

"This is ridiculous," she muttered as she put Emmie's coat on her, then stuffed her arms into the sleeves of her own.

Josh Gordon was the very last man she should be shivering over. He couldn't be trusted. He might have given her a month's worth of extra funds for the day care center, but that didn't fool her for a second. She had overheard enough comments from some of the other members to know that he would like to see it fail—almost as much as Beau Hacket and Paul Windsor did.

So what was he up to? And why?

Three

When Josh entered the bar, he looked around to see if any of his friends had stopped by for happy hour since it appeared he was going to be spending his evening hanging out with the guys. Not exactly what he had planned. He had intended to have an early dinner with Kiley at the exclusive new restaurant across town, lay to rest what happened that night three years ago and convince her that he fully intended to give her day care center a fair evaluation.

Why her opinion of him mattered was still a mystery to him. He had never before cared one way or the other what others thought of him. As long as he based his decisions on what he knew was right, he could sleep at night. But for some reason it bothered him that Kiley obviously had such little faith in his integrity. Why would she think he would stoop so low as to let her not going to dinner with him influence his recommendations to the funding committee? More importantly, why couldn't he just let it go?

Normally once he discovered a woman had a child, his interest in her took a nosedive and he moved on. But for some strange reason, Kiley and her daughter piqued his curiosity. Why would any man in his right mind willingly walk away from either of them?

"Hey, Josh," someone called, drawing him out of his introspection.

Spotting the current TCC president, Gil Addison, seated on the far side of the room, Josh threaded his way through the crowd. "I didn't expect to see you here, Gil," he said when he reached the table.

"Cade was invited to have dinner with one of his friends from the day care center." Gil shrugged. "I was just trying to decide whether to go home and raid the refrigerator or stay here and order something."

"Mind if I join you?" Josh asked. "My plans for dinner fell through at the last minute."

Grinning, Gil motioned toward the empty chair across from him. "Have a seat. I can't remember how long it's been since I had a meal that wasn't business-related or kid-dominated."

"You've had a pretty full plate since becoming president," Josh agreed, pulling out the chair to sit down.

A single father, Gil Addison was totally devoted to his small son, and he wasn't often seen having a beer with other members in the club's bar just for fun. It was nice to see his friend enjoying a little downtime for a change.

"Hi, I'm Ginny. I'll be your server tonight. What can I get for you two?" a tall, dark-haired waitress asked, placing cocktail napkins in front of them in anticipation of a drink order. "We have a steak and fries plate that's out of this world, it's so good."

"I'll have that and a beer," Josh spoke up.

"Might as well double that order," Gil added.

"Great choice," Ginny said, jotting their orders on a pad of paper. "I'll be right back with your beer."

While they waited on Ginny to return with their drinks, Josh and Gil talked about how the club membership had grown with the addition of women to its roster.

"I know some of the older members have a problem with it," Gil said, shrugging. "But the Texas Cattleman's Club needs to be progressive in its thinking and recognize that this isn't the same club Tex Langley founded around the turn of the last century. The 'good old boy network' was fine a hundred-plus years ago, but it just isn't practical in today's world."

"I have to admit, I've had my share of misgivings about women belonging to the club," Josh said honestly. "But after working with Nadine Capshaw since she was appointed to the funding committee last month, it's given me a new perspective on the issue. I think my main concerns now revolve around some of the changes the women are lobbying for. It seems at times that the TCC is heading toward becoming more of a country club than an organization that has always set the bar with its dedication to serving the needs of the community of Royal."

They both fell silent when the waitress brought them mugs of beer.

"I understand your and some of the other members' concerns," Gil said when Ginny moved away to serve another table. "And I know that some of the additions being made to the club's services for our members are viewed as unnecessary. But the way I see it, the more opportunities we offer, the better the chance our membership will stay strong and enable us to continue assisting the community."

"I guess you have a point," Josh conceded. He waited until Ginny had set their plates of food in front of them before he continued. "Speaking of our services, how do you like the new day care center? Is it living up to your expectations for your son?"

"It's exceeded them," Gil answered, cutting into his steak. "Cade looks forward to being with his friends each day and it's a load off my mind, knowing that while I conduct TCC business, he's being looked after right down the hall."

"The director seems to be pretty good with kids," Josh said, taking a bite of his steak.

Gil nodded. "Kiley Roberts is amazing. I can't believe some of the things Cade has learned since starting at the day care center last month." He smiled fondly as he talked about his son. "He can tie his own shoes now and is able to recognize a few basic words when he sees them."

"That's pretty good for a four-year-old, isn't it?" Josh asked. He really didn't know if it was or not. But then he didn't know much about what little kids learned at any age.

"Kiley has a real way with kids. She makes a game out of learning and they soak it up like sponges." Gil grinned. "Even getting Cade to go to bed is easier because she told them how important it is to get plenty of rest at night so they can play with their friends the next day."

Josh finished his dinner and took a drink of his beer. "She's asked for more money from the funding committee and I've been stopping by the center to see what the funds would be used for, and to determine whether I should recommend increasing the day care's yearly budget."

"Yeah, I heard Beau grousing about it the other day." Gil paused for a moment. "I know the decision to appropriate more money to the day care center's budget is entirely up to the funding committee. But for what it's worth, I think it would be money well spent." Something on one of the many televisions around the bar suddenly caught his attention. "Damn!"

Josh looked up to see a picture of Alex Santiago on one of the national evening news broadcasts. The anchorman reported that although Alex had been found, the investigation into his mysterious disappearance was ongoing. The reporter asked that anyone having seen Alex during the months he had been missing to please contact the state investigator, Britt Collins. He wrapped up the segment with a statement that all leads were being followed and that several members of the prestigious Texas Cattleman's Club had been questioned as persons of interest in the case.

Clearly angered by the report, Gil shook his head. "I don't like that the TCC is being disparaged by any of this. Our reputation has always been impeccable and every member of the club is carefully screened before they're granted membership. This Collins woman has already interrogated Chance McDaniel, Dave Firestone and myself. Who's she going to single out next?"

"It's my guess she'll investigate every one of us if she has to," Josh said, finishing his beer. "I've heard she's quite thorough."

"She'd do well to look elsewhere for possible suspects," Gil stated flatly.

Josh motioned for the waitress to bring their checks. "I wouldn't worry too much about the TCC's reputation. We've always been above reproach. We can weather this and anything else that casts a shadow of doubt over our integrity."

"You're right, but the club has been the subject of more than one negative news report lately," Gil reminded.

"Have there been any more leads in the vandalism of the day care center?" Josh asked, picking up the slip of paper the waitress placed facedown in front of him. "The last I heard the police think it might have been teenagers."

"That's what I heard, too." Gil reached for his check. "They're the only ones I can think of that might be stupid enough to mess with the TCC. The lead detective did tell me they found a partial fingerprint, but when they ran it through the national database there weren't any matches. He thinks it might be one of the members' kids."

Josh nodded as he removed his wallet from the inside pocket of his suit coat and tossed several dollars on the table to cover his dinner and a generous tip. "Kids are the only ones stupid enough to do something like this. Anyone else knows better than to come into our house and destroy any part of it. But you'd think a kid of one of our members wouldn't even think about it."

"Well, whoever it is, they've bit off more than they realize," Gil agreed. "I personally can't think of a single member, no matter what they think of the day care center, who doesn't want them held accountable for what they've done." Checking his watch, he rose to leave. "I guess I'd better get over to the Whelans' and pick up Cade. Thanks for sharing dinner with me, Josh."

Rising to his feet, Josh followed his friend out of the bar and walked to his car in favor of having the valet bring it to him. On the drive home, he thought a lot on what Gil had said about the day care center. It was true that the more the TCC had to offer, the better the chances of maintaining a full roster of members. And after seeing the way Kiley dealt with the kids, he knew firsthand that she was good at her job and the day care center was top-notch. Had he been looking at the club's need for a child care facility through jaded eyes?

Josh had to admit it was highly possible. He and his twin brother, Sam, had been raised by a man who made no secret that he thought a woman's place was in the home taking care of her own children and not outside of it working a job or playing tennis while someone else looked after her kids. For the most part, he had agreed with their father and it wasn't until he'd watched Kiley work with the kids that he was starting to question his steadfast opinion.

Maybe his thinking would have been different if his mother had lived long enough to really have an influence on his and Sam's lives. But other than what he saw from the pictures his dad had shown him,

Josh couldn't honestly say he recalled much about his mother.

Turning his car up the long drive leading to his ranch house, he decided to take Alex's advice and not make any rash decisions about his recommendation to the funding committee. He had the rest of the month to observe what went on at the day care center and he owed it to Kiley, as well as the members of the TCC, to give it a fair evaluation before he decided one way or the other.

On Saturday afternoon when Kiley parked in front of Josh's barn, her pulse sped up as she watched him walk toward her car. If she had thought he looked good yesterday when he stopped by the day care center, it couldn't compare to the way he looked today. In a suit and tie the man looked very handsome. In worn jeans, a blue chambray shirt, boots and a wide-brimmed black cowboy hat, he was downright devastating. Who knew he had been hiding such wide shoulders and narrow hips beneath the expensive fabric of those Armani suits?

"Right on time," he said, smiling as he opened her car door for her. "Good, you're wearing jeans."

Silently chastising herself for her wayward thoughts about the man, she took a deep breath and got out of the car. "You didn't think I'd wear heels and a dress to walk through a feedlot, did you?"

He laughed. "You wore a dress the other day."

"That's because I was going before your committee to ask for more money for the day care center," she said, turning to open the back door of the car. "You've seen me in slacks and a blouse every time since then."

The look in his blue gaze stole her breath. "And you've looked very nice in everything I've seen you in."

Surprised by the compliment, she didn't even think to protest when he gently moved her out of the way, opened the rear door, then unbuckled the safety straps and lifted her daughter from the car seat. "Are you ready to ride a horse, Emmie?" he asked.

Seated on his forearm, Emmie clapped her little hands together. "Me wide ponies."

"You didn't say anything about riding," Kiley accused, glaring at him. He knew she hadn't wanted to pay him a visit to begin with, let alone spend more time with him by going for a horseback ride.

"I didn't think of it until just a short while ago." He smiled at her happy daughter. "I thought this little lady might enjoy it."

"I'm sure she would," Kiley said without thinking. As soon as the words passed her lips, she knew she'd made a huge mistake and played right into his hands.

Josh gave her a triumphant grin as he placed his free hand to the small of her back. "Then it's settled."

"You're manipulating the situation, the same as you did yesterday afternoon," she said tightly as he guided her toward the corral where two saddled horses stood, their reins tied to the top rail of the fence.

"Not really." He opened the gate to the corral and led her over to a pinto mare. "I wasn't sure how experienced you are with horses, so I had my foreman saddle Daisy. She's the most gentle horse I own. You can ride, can't you?"

"Yes, but it's been a while since I've had the opportunity," Kiley admitted, patting the horse's neck.

"Do you need help mounting?" Josh asked from behind her.

She shook her head as she untied the reins and raised her leg to mount up. "I think I can manage."

Unfortunately, she was short and the horse was quite tall. When she put her foot in the stirrup, her knee was even with her chin and made it all but impossible to pull herself up into the saddle.

"Here, let me help," Josh said.

Before she realized what he intended, she felt his hand cup her backside and, as if she weighed nothing, he gave her the boost she needed to mount the mare. Her cheeks felt as if they were on fire when she settled herself in the saddle. Thankfully her daughter provided the distraction Kiley needed to regain her composure.

"Pony," Emmie said delightedly, touching the mare's mane.

When Kiley reached for her, Emmie stubbornly shook her head and put her arms around Josh's neck. "Wide a pony."

"You're going to ride a pony with me," Kiley explained.

Her daughter's blond pigtails swayed as she shook her head. "No!"

"Emmie," Kiley warned, keeping her tone firm but gentle.

Her little chin began to wobble and tears filled her big brown eyes. "No, pease."

"She can ride with me," Josh offered softly.

Emmie nodded her head. "Wide."

Kiley wasn't happy, but she finally nodded her consent. It wasn't that she didn't think Josh would keep her daughter safe. It was a matter of Emmie becoming too attached to him. She had watched her little girl's reaction when some of the children's fathers arrived at the end of the day to take them home and it was clear Emmie missed a paternal influence in her life.

As Kiley watched Josh untie the reins of the bay gelding and effortlessly swing up into the saddle while still holding Emmie, her heart ached. Her daughter deserved to have two parents, but it hadn't worked out that way and there was no sense lamenting the fact that she didn't.

"Me wide pony," Emmie said happily when Josh settled her on his lap and nudged his horse into a slow walk.

By the time they rode through the gate into the pasture beyond, Kiley had to admit that although she had been against the outing and still resented the way Josh had controlled everything, she wouldn't have missed the excitement on Emmie's face for anything. Her little girl was having the time of her life.

"She seems to be enjoying herself," Josh said, smiling when Emmie braced both hands on the saddle horn and grinned over her shoulder at him.

Kiley nodded. "She's always loved animals, but horses and ponies are her favorites. Even before she could sit up on her own, she had a stuffed pony that she wouldn't let out of her sight."

"Does her dad like horses?" he asked. "Maybe that's where she gets it from."

"No, he hasn't been in the picture since right after she was born," Kiley said, shrugging.

"I'm sorry," Josh said, sounding sincere.

"Don't be." She stared off into the distance. "Emmie and I are better off without him."

"He doesn't have any contact at all with you and Emmie?" He sounded disapproving.

Shaking her head, she smiled. "No. Mark signed over all legal rights to her so he wouldn't have to pay child support."

Josh stopped the bay gelding to turn and look at her. "And you're okay with that?"

"Actually, I'm just as glad I don't have to deal with him," she said honestly, reining in the mare. "But it breaks my heart for Emmie. When she gets a little older she'll start wondering why her dad didn't want anything to do with her."

"It's his loss," Josh stated flatly. "He's the one missing out and it sounds to me like the bast—" he stopped, looked down at Emmie, then, grinning, finished "—the jerk doesn't have the sense to know it."

She didn't know why she had opened up to Josh, but it was no secret in Royal that Mark Roberts cared little or nothing for anyone but himself. Of course, he wasn't a part of the same social set as Josh and his friends, so she doubted Josh had ever heard of Mark or his reputation for being his own number one fan.

"I know it's none of my business, but why did you marry him?" Josh asked, frowning.

"You're holding her." Kiley smiled fondly at her pride and joy. "I became pregnant and his grandfather insisted that he had to do the 'right thing' and marry me."

"You didn't have to go along with it," he pointed out.

"It appears that my sister isn't the only one in the

Miller family who makes poor choices when it comes to the men she gets involved with," Kiley said without thinking.

"Ouch."

"Oh, I'm sorry," she said, realizing that Josh thought she meant him. It was true that he had broken Lori's heart, but he was just one of a long list of men Lori had fallen for over the years. "I didn't mean you in particular," she hurried to add. "I just meant Lori seems to always fall for men who are all wrong for her."

He shrugged. "Lori's a great girl. But her attention span isn't all that long."

When he didn't say more, Kiley wondered what he meant by that comment. Lori wasn't known for seeing anyone for very long, but he made it sound as if she was the one who'd dumped him instead of the other way around. But Lori had said…

"That's why you said the day care center was your dream job," he said, drawing Kiley back to the present. "As long as you have to work to support yourself and Emmie, it's better to have her with you."

"By having her with me, I don't have to worry about missing any of her childhood milestones or wonder if someone else is taking good care of her," Kiley said, nodding.

He looked thoughtful, as if mulling over what she had told him before glancing down at Emmie. "Uh-oh. It looks like this little cowgirl is going to miss part of the ride."

When she looked over at her daughter leaning back against Josh, she smiled. Emmie was fast asleep.

"I think it was probably the rhythmic movement of the gelding's slow walk and the fact that she has been extremely excited about seeing the horses. When the adrenaline level starts to drop off, the little ones are usually asleep in no time." She stopped the mare. "Do you want me to take her?"

Smiling, he shook his head. "No, she's fine. Besides, I'd hate to wake her."

They fell silent as they rode along a creek on the far side of the pasture before turning back. Maybe Josh wasn't such a bad guy after all, Kiley decided.

As they rode across the wide pasture, Kiley found herself glancing at Josh holding her daughter securely to his wide chest and a warm feeling began to fill her. Was there ever a more endearing sight than a man tenderly holding a child?

When she remembered how surrounded she'd felt with his chest pressed to hers and the latent strength of his arms holding her close as he made love to her that night, a streak of longing coursed through her at the speed of light. Her heart skipped a beat and she had to remind herself to breathe. Where had that come from? And what on earth was wrong with her?

Josh Gordon was the very last man her heart should be fluttering over. If he and some of the other funding committee members had their way about it, the day care center would close and she would be out of a job—her dream job. She would be much better off focusing on that than to be thinking about how passionate he had been or how cherished she'd felt when he'd made love to her.

When he and Kiley rode the horses back into the corral, Josh was careful not to wake Emmie as he dismounted the bay. He had never before noticed how cute a little kid was when they were sleeping. Of course, he hadn't been around kids enough to know whether they all looked innocent and sweet or if it was just Emmie.

How in the name of hell could Roberts have walked away from her and Kiley? Why hadn't he at least wanted to be a big part of his kid's life?

Josh shook his head as he turned to help Kiley down from the mare. "Emmie's going to be disappointed that she slept through most of her first horseback ride."

Kiley nodded as she took Emmie from him and lifted her daughter to her shoulder. "Thank you, Josh. She really enjoyed it while she was awake and she'll be talking about petting the horses for days."

The sound of her soft voice saying his name and the sweet smile she gave him caused a warmth like nothing he had ever known to rush through him. He had to clear his throat before he could speak. "It was my pleasure, Kiley. We'll have to do it again soon. Maybe Emmie will be able to stay awake through the entire ride next time."

Emmie stirred against Kiley's shoulder and, raising her head, sleepily looked around. "Ponies." When she realized the ride was over, tears filled her eyes and she looked as if her heart had been broken. "Wide… a pony."

Josh felt like he'd taken a piece of candy or a favorite toy from her. "Do you mind if I hold her on the saddle while I lead the horses into the barn?" he asked Kiley. "You know, give her a little more riding time?"

"No, I don't mind," she said, wiping a big tear from Emmie's round little cheek. "Would you like for Josh to give you another ride on the pony?"

Emmie nodded and held both of her arms out for him to take her. "Wide a pony."

Without a moment's hesitation, he took her from her mother and set her on the gelding's saddle. "Hold on to the saddle horn," he instructed, showing her where to put her hands. Emmie gave him a smile that he wouldn't have missed for anything. "We'll come back for the mare," he said, turning to Kiley. "That way, she'll get to ride twice."

Putting his arm around Emmie to make sure she didn't slide off the saddle, Josh loosely held the reins as he urged the gelding into a slow walk. All of his horses had been well-trained and he was confident the animal wouldn't just take off. But he wasn't taking any chances, either.

Once the bay was tied to a grooming post inside the barn, Josh and Emmie returned to the corral to get the mare. From the look on Emmie's face, he had made some major points with her. The child was grinning from ear to ear by the time the mare was tied beside the gelding.

"Bobby Ray, would you start grooming the mare?" Josh called to his foreman at the far end of the barn. "I'll be back in a few minutes to take care of the bay." Lifting Emmie from the saddle, he walked back out to where Kiley stood by the corral gate, talking to Bobby Ray's wife. "I see you've met my housekeeper, Martha," he said, smiling at the two women.

"Oh, my word," Martha said, her face splitting into a wide grin when she spotted Emmie. "What a beautiful little angel!"

"Would you like for Martha to show you her new kittens?" Josh whispered to Emmie as if they were sharing a big secret. For reasons he didn't want to dwell on, he wanted to prolong her and Kiley's departure.

"Wanna see kitties," Emmie said happily.

"Is it all right to take her to see the two kittens we adopted from the animal shelter?" Martha asked Kiley.

"That would be fine," Kiley answered, smiling. "I'm sure she would like that."

When Josh set Emmie on her feet, she readily took Martha's hand and waved at him and her mother. "Bye."

"She's a great kid," Josh said, watching his housekeeper and Emmie walk back into the barn.

"Thanks."

"I feel like I should be the one thanking you," he said truthfully. "I've really enjoyed getting to see the wonder on her face."

Kiley nodded. "Every day is a big adventure for a two-year-old."

"I'm sure it can be an adventure for you, as well," he said, thinking about how difficult it had to be, raising a child with no help.

She laughed. "Well, there have been a couple of times when her adventures have turned into my disasters."

The delightful sound of Kiley's laughter did strange things to his insides and he didn't think twice about reaching out to pull her into his arms. "Thank you for letting me share in Emmie's latest adventure," he said, hugging her close.

Her body pressed to his felt wonderful even through the many layers of their clothing. When she leaned back to look up at him with her luminous brown eyes,

Josh couldn't have stopped himself from kissing her if his life depended on it.

Slowly lowering his head, he gave her the chance to call a halt to things. To his relief, her eyes fluttered shut as his mouth covered hers. Soft and sweet, her lips clung to his, reminding him of that night in her sister's apartment. A spark ignited in his belly and his lower body began to tighten predictably. He had suspected part of the reason that night had gone as far as it did was because of an undeniable chemistry between them. Now he knew for certain he was right. The reality of her response surpassed his memory of that night, and he knew absolutely that a force of nature was at work drawing them together.

Forcing himself to keep the kiss brief and nonthreatening, he eased away from the caress instead of deepening it as he would have liked. "I've been wanting to do that for the past few days," he said, smiling down at her.

Kiley took a quick step back. "Th-that shouldn't... have happened."

"I'll be damned if I'm sorry it did."

"I... We should go," she said, looking a little flustered. Unless he missed his guess, she felt the magnetic pull as strongly as he did and it scared her senseless.

Before either of them could say anything more, Martha and Emmie returned from the barn.

"Me petted kitties," Emmie said excitedly.

"Tell Mr. Gordon thank you for inviting us to see the ponies and the kitties," Kiley said, her gaze not quite meeting his.

"Tank you," Emmie said politely.

Taking the little girl by the hand to lead her to the

car, he smiled. "You're very welcome, Emmie. We'll go for another ride the next time you come back to my ranch. Would you like that?"

The toddler nodded until her curly pigtails bounced. "Yes."

He opened the back door of Kiley's car and lifted Emmie into the car seat. Stepping back, he waited until Kiley buckled the safety straps and closed the car door before he reached up to brush a strand of blond hair from her smooth cheek.

"Drive safe."

She nodded as she hurriedly turned to get in behind the steering wheel. "I'll see you next week at the day care center."

"Yeah," he said, smiling confidently as he watched her turn the car around and start back up the drive to the main road. "You'll see me before then, too."

He had forgotten to tell Kiley about the partial fingerprint the detectives had found when they investigated the vandalism at the day care center and that after running it through their database, they had concluded the perpetrator didn't have a criminal record. It wasn't anything that couldn't wait until he saw her at the day care center, but as far as he was concerned it was reason enough to pay her a visit that evening. Besides, they still had yet to discuss their night together, and she might be more inclined to talk about what happened in the privacy of her own home.

Whistling a tune, he walked back to the barn to help his ranch foreman finish grooming the horses. Now that he had plans for the evening, he suddenly couldn't wait to get them started.

Four

Driving across town after picking up a pizza, Josh thought about what Kiley had told him earlier that afternoon while they were riding his horses. She had never received help from her ex-husband. As chairman of the funding committee, he knew exactly what her salary was. The TCC paid her the going rate for a day care center director, but it wasn't something she would ever get rich from. In fact, he wouldn't be the least bit surprised if she was struggling to make ends meet.

Suddenly several things became quite clear, causing a knot to form in his gut. Kiley had called working at the day care center her dream job. But aside from being able to be with Emmie, she needed to keep her position for two very important reasons. She needed to provide for herself and Emmie, and she probably couldn't afford the rising cost of child care if she worked any other job.

Now he felt guilty as hell for being so closed-minded about the day care center. To a certain degree he had been on the same page with Beau Hacket and Paul Windsor. His father had raised him and his twin with the misguided belief that a woman's place was in the home, taking care of her own kids. Period.

But what they had all failed to take into consideration was the fact that women not only had the right to enjoy recreational activities the same as men, but that some women didn't have a choice but to be out in the workforce. They had to hold a job to help their families make ends meet or, as was Kiley's case, be her family's only support.

Determined to be more open-minded in the future, he turned into the entrance of a subdivision and started watching street signs for Cottonwood Lane. It seemed to be a nice enough neighborhood, but he could tell that it was older and some of the houses were in desperate need of repairs, if not a complete renovation.

When he turned onto Kiley's street, he hadn't gone far when he spotted her older Ford sedan parked in the driveway of a small bungalow. He pulled his Mercedes in behind her car. The lights were on inside the house and he would bet that she and Emmie were probably getting ready for dinner.

"Right on time," he said, grabbing the pizza box and getting out of his car.

Walking up to the front door, he rang the bell and waited. When Kiley opened the door, his heart stalled and he couldn't believe how hard it was to take in his next breath. Dressed in a pink T-shirt that gave him a pretty fair idea of the size and shape of her breasts, and black leggings that hugged her slender legs like a second skin, she could easily tempt a saint to sin.

He forced himself to give her what he hoped was an innocent smile as he presented the pizza. "Dinner is served."

She looked confused. "Josh, what are you doing here?"

"I thought you'd be tired after today's outing and might not feel like cooking," he said suddenly, wondering if he'd lost his mind. It was clear Kiley was trying to keep him at arm's length. Why couldn't he accept that?

Emmie peeked out from behind her mother's legs. As soon as she recognized him, she started looking around the yard. "Ponies. Wanna wide ponies."

"I'm sorry, Emmie. The horses were tired and I left them at my ranch to rest," he said, hoping it was a good enough explanation for a two-year-old. He held out the box for her to see. "But I brought pizza for dinner."

The temptation of pizza worked its magic and, grinning, the little girl clapped her tiny hands. "Petza."

Kiley didn't look happy. "I normally make sure she has a more healthy dinner."

"I thought of that," he said, rocking back on his heels. "That's why I ordered the vegetable pizza with real cheese on a hand-tossed, whole-grain crust."

He was actually pretty proud of himself for thinking of the nutritional value for a change. Normally, when he had pizza it was loaded with meat, there wasn't the hint of a vegetable on it and the crust was as thick as a slice of Texas toast.

"Petza, Mommy," Emmie said, tugging on the tail of Kiley's T-shirt.

"Oh, all right," she finally said, stepping back.

When he entered the house, Josh looked around. It was exactly as he thought it would be—very warm and homey. The furniture was older and a bit worn, but everything was neat and clean, and looked very comfortable.

Noticing a couple of place mats on the coffee table, he raised an eyebrow. "Dinner in front of the TV?"

"Saturday is movie night for Emmie and me," Kiley explained. "I was just about to make tuna sandwiches." Walking into the kitchen, she returned to put another place mat down on the coffee table along with three small plates. "Would you like a glass of iced tea? I'm sorry I don't have anything stronger."

"I'll have whatever you're having," he said, placing the pizza box on the table with the plates. He waited until she returned with two glasses of iced tea and a small cup of milk with a straw built into the lid. "What are we watching this evening?"

"A classic cartoon about a mermaid princess who wants to be a real girl," Kiley said, dishing up slices of pizza. "It's one of Emmie's favorites."

Their fingers brushed when she handed him his plate, and it felt like a jolt of electric current traveled up his arm and exploded somewhere around his solar plexus. As quickly as she jerked her hand back, Josh knew beyond a shadow of doubt that she had felt it, too.

"Me pincess," Emmie said, nodding as Kiley fastened a bib around her neck to protect her pink footed pajamas with fairy-tale princesses on them. It was obvious the toddler was ready for bed and Josh would bet his last dollar that she fell asleep well before the movie was over.

While her mother cut the slice of pizza on her plate into little pieces, Emmie suddenly took off running down the hall.

"Where did she go?" he asked, confused.

Kiley smiled. "She's going to show you that she's a real princess."

When the little girl returned, she was wearing a gold-colored plastic crown with jewels painted on it. It was a little too large for her head and it kept sliding to one side, but she wore it as proudly as if it were the Crown Jewels.

"Me pincess," she said again as she picked up one of the bite-size pieces of pizza and put it into her mouth.

"Yes, you are," Josh said, unable to stop smiling. For some reason, he found everything the kid did to be cute as hell, and he was fascinated by her enthusiasm and delight in the simplest of things.

When he caught Kiley staring at him, he frowned. "What?"

"N-nothing," she said, picking up the remote control. Pushing a couple of buttons, she started the DVD and in no time Emmie became completely engrossed in the cartoon.

As they ate, he noticed Kiley glancing at him and then Emmie several times, but she remained strangely silent. Before he could ask her what was wrong, she paused the DVD player.

"If you'll excuse us, I need to finish getting her ready for bed," she said, taking Emmie by the hand.

While she took her daughter down the hall to the bathroom to wash her face and hands and brush her teeth, Josh took their plates and the empty pizza box into the kitchen. When he returned to the living room, he had barely settled himself on the couch when Emmie came running in to climb up on the cushion beside him.

Grinning up at him, she jabbered something that he assumed meant she wanted him to start the movie again. Fortunately Kiley was right behind her. Maybe she could translate toddler speak.

"Does she want me to start the movie again?" he asked, wondering why Kiley had stopped just inside the room. She looked as if she'd seen a ghost. "Is something wrong?"

His question seemed to snap her out of whatever she'd been thinking and, giving him a slight smile, she shook her head. "Please go ahead and take the player off Pause."

When Kiley started to sit in the armchair, Emmie shook her head and, getting down, took hold of her mother's hand. "Mommy," she said determinedly, tugging Kiley toward the couch.

"I think she wants you to sit with us," Josh said, deciding he owed the kid a debt of gratitude.

Kiley didn't look all that happy about it, but she did as her daughter wanted, and after Emmie climbed up beside him, she sat down on the other side of the little girl to finish watching the cartoon. Within ten minutes, Emmie surprised him yet again when she crawled over to sit on his lap and lean back against his chest.

Kiley started to move to the opposite end of the couch, but Josh put his arm around her shoulders to stop her. "The princess is about to go to sleep. If you move, it might disturb her," he whispered close to her ear.

He felt a tremor course through her before she gave him an exasperated look. "What are you doing, Josh?"

"Watching the movie with you and Emmie."

"You know what I mean," she said, shaking her head.

"Could we discuss this after she goes to sleep?" he asked, stalling.

The truth was, he didn't know why he felt the need to get close to Kiley. Normally women with little kids were the last females he wanted to get close to. But that wasn't the case with Kiley. Maybe it was that night three years ago that compelled him, or it could be the fact that the more he learned about her and her daughter, the more he wanted to know. He wasn't sure. But he had always followed his gut instinct and it was telling him not to be too hasty—to take his time and explore what was drawing him to them.

"She's asleep," Kiley said quietly as she reached for Emmie.

"If you'll lead the way, I'll carry her for you," Josh said, cradling the toddler to him as he rose to his feet. "She's as limp as cooked spaghetti."

Kiley's soft laughter caused a warm feeling to spread throughout his chest. "Children don't have the stress adults have. When they fall asleep they're completely relaxed."

Following her down the hall to Emmie's room, he placed the little girl on the smallest bed he had ever seen. He waited for Kiley out in the hall while she pulled the covers over Emmie and kissed her goodnight.

"I didn't know they made beds that little," he said when they walked back into the living room.

"It's a toddler bed." She turned off the DVD player

and removed the disk. "Emmie is too old for a crib and too little for a twin-size bed."

"That makes sense."

Staring at him for a moment, she finally asked, "Why did you come by tonight, Josh?"

"I forgot to mention this afternoon that the detective in charge of the vandalism case told Gil Addison that they analyzed a fingerprint found at the day care center," he stated.

"Were they able to find out who it belonged to?"

He shook his head. "It didn't match anyone in their database, so whoever was behind the destruction doesn't have a criminal record."

Kiley straightened the afghan on the back of the couch. "I was hoping by now the authorities would have someone in custody or at least have an idea of who the person was."

"From all indications, they think it might be a couple of the TCC members' kids," Josh said from behind her.

"And this couldn't have waited until Monday?" When Kiley turned to face him, her heart skipped a beat. He was way too close for comfort.

His slow grin sent goose bumps shimmering over her skin. "It probably could have, but I wanted to see you again."

"We spent the afternoon with you. Wasn't that enough?" she asked, wishing her voice didn't sound so darned breathless.

Slowly reaching out, he put his arms around her. She knew he was intentionally giving her a chance to back away, but for the life of her, she couldn't seem to get her feet to move.

"No, it wasn't enough," he said, smiling. "I wasn't able to give you a proper goodbye kiss this afternoon."

"Josh, it wasn't a good idea then and it's an even worse idea now." Why couldn't she make her tone sound more convincing?

"Why do you say that, Kiley?" he asked, brushing his mouth over hers.

"I… Well…it just…is," she said, sounding anything but sure. She needed time to think, but he was making it impossible.

As she stared up into his darkening blue eyes, he lowered his mouth to hers and any protest she was about to make went right out the window. She had tried for the past three years to forget how his lips felt moving over hers, how masterful his kiss was. It had been a subtle reminder when he'd kissed her earlier that afternoon at his ranch. But that paled in comparison to the way he was kissing her now.

Tasting and teasing, he traced her mouth with his tongue until she parted her lips on a soft sigh. When he slipped inside to gently explore her inner recesses, a delicious heat began to slowly glide its way through her and her knees suddenly felt as if they were made of rubber. When she raised her arms to his shoulders, he caught her to him, and the feel of his hard masculine body pressed against her softer form felt absolutely wonderful. It had been so very long since she'd been held by a man, felt the carefully controlled strength of his caress and the excitement of his lips claiming hers.

Lost in the delicious feelings, it took a moment for her to realize that Josh had brought his hand up to cup her breast. Even through her clothing the feel of his thumb chafing the tight tip caused a tingling sensation to travel straight to the most feminine part of her. A longing like nothing she'd ever known threatened to swamp her.

The ringing of her phone suddenly broke through the sensual haze Josh had created and helped to restore some of her sanity. Pulling from his arms, her hand trembled when she reached to pick up the cordless unit. She immediately recognized her sister's number on the caller ID.

"I-It's…Lori. I'll…call her back…in a few minutes," she said, struggling to catch her breath. "You should probably…go, Josh."

Josh stared at her for several long seconds before he finally nodded. "Tell Lori I said hello." He started for the door, then, turning back, reached up to run his index finger along her cheek. "I know that you're reluctant to acknowledge that it even exists, but whatever this is between us hasn't diminished. If anything, it's stronger now than it was that night."

"Josh—"

Giving her a quick kiss, he opened the front door. "I'll see you Monday afternoon."

Unable to form a coherent sentence, Kiley watched him leave before she sank down on the couch. Her head was still spinning from his kiss, but it was what she had noticed when she watched him and Emmie together that made her feel as if the rug had been pulled out from under her.

She had always thought that Emmie looked like her. They both had the same hair and eye color. But watching Josh and her daughter together, Kiley had noticed several similarities that had her questioning everything she thought she was sure of. Emmie had the same smile as Josh, the same patrician nose, and although her eyes were brown instead of blue, they were the same shape as his.

Shaking her head to clear it, Kiley rose from the couch and wandered into the spare bedroom she used for an office. Sitting down at the desk, she booted up her laptop and brought up a website that she hoped would prove that she'd lost her mind.

A half hour later, Kiley stared off into space as the gravity of her findings sank in. She had calculated everything twice and there was no way to deny it. There was a very real possibility that, instead of her ex-husband, Josh Gordon was Emmie's father.

Kiley waited until the following morning to call her sister back. She was still trying to come to terms with the probability of Josh being Emmie's father. But the more she thought about it, the more it explained.

Emmie looked absolutely nothing like Mark. He had an olive complexion, black hair and a distinct Roman nose. Nothing like her daughter's facial features. And then there were the numbers that added up against Mark being her father.

Kiley had always thought she became pregnant a few weeks later, when she and Mark patched things up after that night in her sister's apartment. But the more she thought about it, the less likely that was the date she had conceived. If she calculated Emmie's birth by that, Emmie had been born three weeks early. But when she calculated it by the night she and Josh made love, Emmie had arrived right on time.

She knew that wasn't conclusive proof. Only a DNA test would be proof positive. But everything added up to suggest that Josh was more likely Emmie's father than Mark.

Deciding that she would end up completely over-whelmed by it all if she didn't distract herself, she di-aled her sister's number. "Hi, Lori," Kiley said when her sister answered the phone. "I'm sorry I missed your call last night. I was…um, busy."

"No problem," Lori said cheerfully. "I figured you were probably having trouble getting my adorable niece tucked in for the night."

"Saturday nights are easy. Emmie always falls asleep during the movie and it's just a matter of car-rying her to bed," Kiley said, wondering how she was going to bring up the subject of Lori's relationship with Josh. From what he had said about Lori being a great girl, it didn't sound like the breakup had been as disastrous as her sister had described at the time.

"I tried calling yesterday afternoon to see if you wanted to go help me start my Christmas shopping, but you weren't home." Lori laughed. "You know me. I always wait until the last minute to buy gifts for ev-eryone and I need your opinion. Otherwise, I go into panic mode and buy something completely inappro-priate for everyone." It was so typical of Lori. She had procrastination down to an art form.

"I put all of the gifts I'm giving into layaway this past fall." Kiley smiled. "It doesn't feel as expensive when I pay a little out of each paycheck and I'm able to put a little more thought into what I'm giving."

"You always were the smart one of the Miller girls," Lori said, laughing.

"There are only two of us," Kiley reminded.

"Just ask Mom and Dad, they'll tell you I'm not the

brightest bulb in the chandelier," Lori said. "Especially when it comes to men."

"Did you break up with your latest boyfriend?" Kiley asked, not at all surprised. Lori's relationships never seemed to last more than a few months.

"No, Sean and I are actually doing quite well," Lori said, sounding amazed. "We've even started talking about moving in together."

"Maybe he's Mr. Right," Kiley said, hoping her sister could find someone who loved her in spite of her flightiness.

"I'm actually thinking he might be," Lori said, sounding extremely hopeful.

"By the way, you'll never guess who I've been having to work with on funding for the day care center," Kiley said, hoping Lori would volunteer some information about her breakup with Josh.

"Who?" Lori asked, her interest obviously piqued.

"Josh Gordon," Kiley stated, awaiting her sister's reaction.

"Oh, Josh is very nice," Lori said, sounding sincere. She laughed suddenly. "In fact, he's one of Royal's most eligible bachelors. I think the two of you should get together. You'd make a really great couple and you need to start dating again."

"I'm not in the market to be part of a couple now or in the future," Kiley said, shaking her head. She knew her sister was teasing her, but she wasn't in the mood.

"That's a shame, because Josh really is a terrific guy," Lori stated.

Kiley frowned. "Now, hold it. Didn't you tell Mom and Dad that he broke your heart when he ended things with you?"

There was a long pause before her sister answered. "Well, it didn't exactly happen the way I told Mom and Dad. You know they're convinced that I make some pretty poor choices in my relationships."

"It must run in the family," Kiley muttered, unable to stop herself.

"Hey, Mark Roberts was the only guy you dated that they didn't approve of," Lori reminded her. "And we both know they were right about him."

Kiley took a deep breath. She didn't want to discuss her brief marriage. "Tell me the real story behind your breakup with Josh."

"We had been dating for a couple of months, but there were times when we'd go for a week or so without seeing each other." Lori paused, then went on. "You know me. I got bored. I sort of started going out with someone else and everything was going great. I saw Josh when we could get together and the other guy when we couldn't." She sighed audibly. "At least, everything was going great until Josh caught us."

"Lori!"

"I know, it was a dumb thing to do," her sister said, sounding contrite. "When Josh found out I was seeing this other guy, I begged him to let me tell Mom and Dad that he was the one who lost interest and ended things between us."

"Why?"

"Because I didn't want to listen to them tell me that I'd screwed up again." Lori sighed. "Josh and I both knew it wasn't a forever kind of relationship from the beginning. When I asked him to help me save face by going along with me telling everyone that he'd found someone else and dumped me, he was really nice and agreed."

Kiley couldn't believe what she'd just heard. "So all this time, we've been thinking that he's a snake in an Armani suit, when in fact he was innocent of doing anything wrong?"

"That just about sums it up," Lori admitted. "Please don't tell Mom and Dad. Things are going great with Sean and I and I'd rather not have strained relations with them when I take him to meet them at the end of this week."

"Don't worry. It's your place to tell them what really happened—not mine," Kiley assured her sister. "I've never been a tattletale and I'm not going to start now. But Josh doesn't deserve their condemnation and they deserve to know the truth. You really should set the record straight." She didn't like lying to anyone, but especially not to their parents.

"I know, and I promise I'll confess soon." She paused. "I'd better go. Sean is here to take me to brunch. Give Emmie hugs and kisses for me."

"I will," Kiley said absently as she ended the call.

How could everything that she'd been so certain about change so quickly?

She had never questioned that Mark was Emmie's father. Hadn't even given it a second thought. But now she knew there was every likelihood that he wasn't. She had also never doubted, until recently, that Josh was the unfeeling jerk who had broken her sister's heart. Finding out that he had been the innocent party in their breakup, yet he'd been generous enough to allow Lori to make him out to be the bad guy in order to save face with their parents, was almost more than Kiley could comprehend.

What else had she been wrong about? And why was she so darned relieved to hear that Josh wasn't a heartbreaking reptile after all?

Five

Josh cursed the weather as he made his way across the ice-covered mud at the job site for the new Duncan Brothers Western Wear store. Hot one week, cold the next, it had been nothing short of bizarre for the past several weeks. But today it had taken a particularly nasty turn. It had been raining since before daylight, but it had only been in the past hour that it started sleeting. With the temperature steadily dropping all day, it had finally reached the freezing point and conditions were deteriorating rapidly. Deciding it was just too dangerous for his men to walk the iron girders of the structure, he'd made the decision to shut the job down for the day and send the crew home. No building was worth risking a man's life.

Climbing into his SUV, he quickly dialed the Gordon Construction offices. "Sam, I've shut down the

Duncan job site and I'm heading home," he said without preamble.

"I figured that was going to happen," his twin brother agreed. "I'm getting ready to go by the clubhouse and pick up Lila, then head home. She had a yoga class at the gym for pregnant mothers and as bad as the roads are getting, I don't want her trying to drive."

Josh didn't blame his brother. Sam's wife, Lila, was only a few months away from having their twins and if Josh had a pregnant wife, he knew he'd be just as cautious.

A sudden thought occurred to him that sent apprehension knifing through him. Kiley and Emmie were at the day care center and wouldn't be able to leave until all of the other kids had been picked up. By that time the roads would be so slick he didn't want to think about what might happen.

"I may see you at the clubhouse," he said, starting his Navigator's powerful engine. It was his work truck and for the first time since he bought it, he was glad it had all-wheel drive. "The day care center's director and her little girl are going to need help getting home."

"Oh…really?" His brother drawled the words. "I didn't think you went for women with kids."

"Can it, bro," Josh said, irritated with his twin. "She lives over in the Herndon subdivision and you know how winding the highway is out that way."

"Yeah, I think the engineer who laid out that road must have been part sidewinder," Sam said, his tone disgusted. "It's bad enough driving that way when the weather's clear, but on days like this it's pure suicide."

"I know. That's why I'm taking them home with

me," he said, instantly making the decision. Just the thought of Kiley and Emmie sliding off into a ditch or, worse yet, into the path of an oncoming car had a knot the size of his fist twisting his gut. "You and Lila be careful getting home."

"We will and the same to you and your new family, Josh," Sam teased.

"Sam, Kiley and I—"

His brother laughed, cutting him off. "Liar. The fact that you're defensive about it tells me these two mean more to you than you're willing to admit."

"Smart-ass," Josh muttered as he ended the call.

He forgot about his brother's observations and concentrated on driving to the clubhouse as fast as it was safe to get there. He wasn't sure, but he would bet anything that parents were picking up their kids early and that Kiley would head home as soon as she could.

Turning on the radio for a weather report, he gritted his teeth at the forecast. The sleet and freezing rain were expected to continue into tomorrow and there were already reports of power outages throughout the region. Kiley's subdivision was one of the areas with no electricity.

He briefly thought about calling her, but decided against it. For one thing, he needed total concentration to keep the truck on the road. And for another, he had a feeling Kiley was going to need some convincing to get her to agree to go to his place.

It seemed as though he'd been on the road for hours by the time he finally made the normally short drive from the job site to the TCC clubhouse. His heart pounded hard against his ribs when he turned into the parking area and it was almost deserted. Had Kiley and Emmie already left?

Looking around for her older sedan, he breathed a sigh of relief when he spotted it on the far side of the parking lot. Hell, just trying to walk on the ice from the front doors of the club all the way over to her car would be more dangerous than it was worth. With a little kid in tow it would be impossible without someone getting hurt.

Josh quickly parked the truck close to the front entrance without blocking it and gingerly walked the short distance across the icy glaze to the doors. Once inside the clubhouse, he quickened his pace and made a beeline down the hall to the day care center.

"How many more kids are left to be picked up?" he asked as he entered the room and found her looking nervously out the window at the coating of ice forming on the children's play area.

"Josh? Why aren't you on your way home? I've heard the roads are really getting treacherous," Kiley said, frowning.

"They are," he answered, looking around. The only other child in the center besides Emmie was Cade Addison. "How long before you're able to leave?"

"Gil is on the way from the president's office to get Cade now," Kiley answered. "I intend to leave as soon as he gets here. Why?"

"I came by to get you and Emmie," he answered, checking his watch. "I'd say we have just enough time to get to my ranch before the highway department closes the roads."

Kiley shook her head. "We're going home."

"This is nonnegotiable, Kiley," he stated flatly. "I

can't in good conscience allow you to drive on the road out to your subdivision."

"Excuse me?" When she turned on him, he realized he'd made a huge mistake. "You can't *allow* me to drive home?"

"Maybe I should rephrase that," he added hastily. "I'm not at all comfortable with the idea of you and Emmie traveling that particular road coated with ice. I'd feel much better about it if you'd let me take you and Emmie to my ranch. It's a lot closer and we'll be off the roads that much sooner."

She shook her head. "I can't do that, Josh."

"Why not?" he demanded, becoming irritated with her stubbornness.

Gil Addison chose that moment to enter the center to get his son, interrupting them. "I hope you both have plans to take off for home as soon as Cade and I leave," he said, helping his son into his coat. "I heard the police are advising people to get off the roads and stay off until the ice storm is over and the highway department gets the roads cleared off."

Josh nodded. "Kiley and I were just discussing that."

"Don't worry about trying to get here to open the day care center for the next couple of days, Kiley," Gil said as he ushered his son toward the door. "I'm closing the clubhouse until the roads are clear, and I anticipate that won't be until closer to the end of the week."

"Thanks for letting me know," she answered. "Please be careful on your way home."

When Gil left, Josh waited until Kiley turned off the lights in her office, grabbed her tote bag and retrieved their coats from the closet. He wasn't about to give up. She would be going home with him.

"On the way over here, I heard that your area of town has already lost power," he reported, hoping he could make her see reason. "Aside from the probability of having an accident on the way home, how are you going to keep Emmie warm for the next several days, provided you could even get there?"

"We would be in the same predicament if you lose electricity," she insisted, looking a little less sure of herself as she zipped up Emmie's coat and tied the hood.

"No, we wouldn't. When I built the house, I had an emergency generator installed. It runs on propane and supplies enough power for the entire house." Deciding they could move faster if he carried her, he reached down to pick up Emmie. "Would you like for me to take you and your mommy home with me to the ranch where the ponies are, Emmie?" he asked the little girl.

It would probably be considered underhanded to use Emmie's love of ponies to get Kiley to go along with him, but so be it. The way he saw it, keeping them safe was a lot more important than playing fair.

"Wanna see ponies," Emmie said, nodding. "Pease!"

Kiley glared at him a moment before she caught her lower lip between her teeth and he could tell she was reviewing her options. "Josh, I'm just not sure it's a good idea. We might be stuck there for several days."

"How many times have you driven on ice?" he asked as they walked out of the day care center and she turned to lock the door.

Making their way down the hall toward the club-house's main entrance, she shook her head. "Since it's extremely rare for us to get weather like this, I can't remember ever driving on it."

"I have and I can tell you that it's no picnic." When they reached the doors, he set Emmie on her feet. "Stay here. I'll go get my SUV and pull it under the canopy so you both stay dry."

"I need to get Emmie's car seat," she said, digging in her tote bag for her car keys.

"There's no sense in either of us breaking our necks trying to walk across a sheet of ice. After I get my truck, I'll drive over to your car and get the car seat." He took her keys from her. "When I come back for you and Emmie, I'll park under the canopy and you can show me how to install it in the backseat."

He had to go so slow that it took several minutes to get to his Navigator and drive over to the other side of the lot in order to retrieve the car seat, then get back to the clubhouse entrance. The SUV kept wanting to fishtail and Josh was more certain than ever that he'd made the right decision to come after Kiley and Emmie.

When he finally drove from under the canopy at the club's front entrance and headed for home, the car seat had been installed, and Kiley and Emmie were safely buckled into their seats. Gripping the steering wheel with both hands, Josh hoped the truck was heavy enough to get at least a little traction, but he wasn't counting on it. Just beyond the TCC's parking lot, a semi hauling a tanker had slid through the intersection and into a deep ravine on the opposite side of the road. If a rig that size had trouble with skidding, what chance did his much lighter SUV have?

Slowly steering the truck out onto the street, Josh didn't draw another breath until he had it straightened out and headed down the highway toward his ranch. The streets were completely deserted, and as they passed car after car off in the ditches lining the road, he decided that although he'd made the right decision about taking Kiley and Emmie to the ranch, it was going to be one hell of a long drive home.

As Josh slowly steered his SUV onto the lane leading up to his ranch house, Kiley finally relaxed enough to unclench her fists. The five-mile trip from the TCC clubhouse to his ranch had taken the better part of an hour and had been more than a little nerve-racking. She had lost count of the vehicles they'd passed that had slid off the road, and there were several times it felt as if the Navigator was going to join them. Fortunately, Josh was an excellent driver and managed to control the truck.

Although she was reluctant to admit it even to herself, she was glad he had insisted that she and Emmie go home with him. There was no way she'd have made it to her subdivision without having an accident. The highway had too many curves, and combined with her inexperience driving on ice, it would have made it impossible not to end up in a ditch. The thought that Emmie might have been hurt caused a chill to snake up her spine.

"Are you cold?" Josh asked, reaching for the heater. "We're almost at the house, but I can turn the heat up if you need me to."

She shook her head. "Thank you, but I'll be fine."

When Josh finally parked the SUV in the attached four-car garage and shut off the engine, he pushed a button on the remote clipped to the driver's sun visor to close the door behind them. "It may have taken a while to get here, but we made it safe and sound."

"Thank you," she said, meaning it. "I can't believe how bad the roads are."

He nodded. "I'm afraid we'll have to make our own dinner. I called Martha earlier this afternoon when the weather started to fall apart and told her and Bobby Ray to go on home. They have a ten-mile drive to their place and I wanted to make sure they got there before the roads got too bad."

Kiley stared at him for a moment. The fact that he was concerned for his housekeeper's and foreman's safety caused her opinion of him to go up several notches.

"I make dinner for Emmie and myself every evening," she said, smiling. "I think I can manage making dinner for the three of us."

He grinned. "Good. I'm afraid my culinary skills only extend as far as boiling water for ramen noodles or packaged macaroni and cheese."

"I thought most Texas men were born knowing how to grill," she teased as she reached for the door handle.

"Wait," he said, getting out of the truck to walk around to her side. Opening the door, he extended his hand to help her down from the seat. "I do know how to grill, but I'm not going to risk life and limb in this weather to walk out to the barbecue pit to burn a couple of steaks."

She laughed. "Where's your sense of adventure?"

"I used it up on that drive home," he said, his smile fading. He reached up to thread his fingers through her hair. "I'm glad you made the decision to come home with me." He leaned down to brush her lips with his.

"I couldn't stand the thought of you trying to navigate all those curves."

Her pulse sped up. "Josh—"

He placed his finger to her mouth to silence her. "I don't want you to worry. Contrary to what happened three years ago, I swear I can be trusted."

Before she could respond, he turned to open the Navigator's back door and reached in to unbuckle Emmie. "She's sound asleep," he whispered, gently lifting her daughter from the car seat.

Kiley's breath caught when Emmie roused, saw who held her, then put her arms around his neck and trustingly laid her head on his shoulder. Her daughter was friendly by nature, but she had never taken to anyone as quickly as she had Josh. Did Emmie somehow sense that he was supposed to be someone special in her life?

Following Josh as he led the way into the house, she couldn't help but wonder what she was going to do about her suspicions that Josh might be Emmie's real father. How was she supposed to even start that conversation? She couldn't very well say, "Oh, by the way, I suspect the child you're holding might be your daughter." That wasn't something just thrown out as a casual comment.

Deciding to keep her silence for the time being in hopes an opportunity presented itself, Kiley followed Josh through the mudroom into the spacious kitchen. When he turned on the lights, she caught her breath as she looked around. The black marble countertops and white custom-made cabinets were gorgeous, but it was the restaurant-size stainless-steel appliances that really caught her eye. They would make cooking an absolute joy.

"This kitchen is a dream come true for anyone who loves to cook," she stated as they continued down a hall to the front foyer. "Do you entertain a lot?"

"I always have our employee Fourth of July barbecue here because I have a bigger yard than my brother." He held Emmie while Kiley removed her sleeping daughter's jacket. "And Sam is in charge of hosting the company Christmas party." He waited until she removed her coat, then handed Emmie to her to take off his. "We sometimes take turns having a couple of dinner parties throughout the year for clients, but that's about it."

While he hung up their coats in a closet close to the front door, Kiley admired the cream-colored marble floor in the foyer and the sweeping staircase leading to the upper level. Everything about Josh's house indicated that he had spared no expense when he'd had it built.

"Hungee," Emmie murmured, waking up to look around.

"Hey there, princess," Josh said, smiling as he closed the closet door.

"Ponies," Emmie said with a shy smile.

Josh laughed and the rich sound did strange things to Kiley's insides. "The ponies are in the barn having their dinner now, but I promise when the weather gets better I'll take you to see them again. Will that be okay?"

Emmie nodded, then put her arms around Kiley's neck. "Hungee, Mommy."

"Then I suppose I'd better find something to make

for dinner," Kiley said, tickling her daughter's tummy. When Emmie dissolved into giggles, she turned to Josh. "Is there anything special you were planning to have Martha make, or should I just search to see what you have?"

"Martha always keeps the refrigerator and pantry fully stocked, so whatever you want to fix is fine with me," he answered. He led the way back to the kitchen. "If you'll tell me what to do, I can probably help a little." He grinned. "And if you need boiling water, I'm your man."

Kiley laughed as she set her tote bag on the kitchen island and reached inside for one of Emmie's ponies. "I'll be sure to remember that." Handing her daughter the toy, she asked, "Could you keep an eye on her while I get started?"

"Do you think she'd like to watch something on TV?" he asked. "I have satellite, as well as access to all kinds of movies and television shows on demand. I'm sure I can find something suitable."

She didn't normally allow Emmie to watch a lot of television, but these weren't normal circumstances. "There is a pony cartoon that I let her watch on occasion."

"I'll find it," Josh promised. Turning to Emmie, he asked, "Would you like to go into the family room with me to see if we can find the pony show on TV?"

"Yes, pease," Emmie said, nodding until her blond pigtails bobbed up and down.

When she watched her child put her little hand in Josh's and walk into the family room with him, Kiley bit her lower lip to keep it from trembling. Her little girl deserved to have a daddy. But how was she going to work up the nerve to share her suspicions with Josh? And if she did manage to find the courage, how receptive would he be? Mark had rejected Emmie, even though he thought she was his child. Would Josh do the same?

"Don't go there," she muttered, shaking her head.

There was one more thing she needed to do that might possibly help her with her decision about talking to Josh. As soon as the weather cleared and things got back to normal, she would call to ask Mark about his blood type. If that ruled out any possibility of him being Emmie's biological father, then she would somehow find the courage to talk to Josh. Until then it would be better to remain silent and turn her attention to a more pressing matter—finding something to make for dinner.

"You're a great cook," Josh said, sitting back from the dining room table. "That was fantastic."

Kiley gave him a smile that sent heat racing through his veins. "I'm glad you liked it, but a simple chicken casserole and some steamed vegetables isn't exactly gourmet fare."

"Would you like to know a little secret about most men?" he asked, grinning.

"Oh, this should be good," she said, laughing. "By all means, please tell me."

Standing, he picked up their plates to carry them to the kitchen, then leaned down to whisper close to her ear. "Most guys really don't care what we eat as long as it's good and there's plenty of it."

She smiled as she wiped off Emmie's face and

hands. "There should be an addendum to that statement."

He arched one eyebrow. "Oh, yeah? What's that?"

"Men really don't care as long as they don't have to cook it," she shot back.

He laughed. "That's a given, honey."

While he put their dishes in the dishwasher, Kiley got Emmie ready for bed. He wasn't sure how other women were with their kids, but Kiley was nothing short of amazing with hers. He couldn't believe how prepared she was. She not only carried toys to entertain Emmie in that tote bag, she also had a change of clothes for her daughter, toddler-size cutlery and an array of healthy snacks.

He decided right then and there that if he ever found himself in a survival situation, he wanted Kiley and her magic tote bag with him. She was prepared for every contingency and managed to get it all in a nice, neat little canvas bag about the size of a large box of cereal.

Walking into the family room to sit down on the couch, he wasn't at all surprised when the lights blinked a couple of times, then went off completely. The generator kicked on automatically and the lights immediately came back on, making him glad that he had thought to add the auxiliary power source when he built the house. The three of them might be stranded until the ice melted, but they would be warm and wouldn't go hungry.

Emmie suddenly came running into the family room as fast as her little legs would carry her. Dressed in the smallest pair of pink sweats he'd ever seen, the little girl's hair was a cloud of damp blond curls around her shoulders and her eyes were wide. She was clearly excited about something. Jumping into this lap, she waved her hands and her big brown eyes sparkled as she jabbered for all she was worth.

"What's she saying?" he asked when Kiley walked in and sat down in the armchair.

Kiley smiled. "She's trying to tell you about the lights going out while she was in the bathtub."

"I promise we won't have to worry about the lights going out again," Josh assured the little girl. He didn't know if she was frightened or just trying to tell him about the experience, but he figured a little reassurance wouldn't hurt.

"Is the house on auxiliary power now?" Kiley asked, putting the clothes Emmie'd had on earlier in the tote bag.

He nodded as he picked up the television's remote control. "I was just getting ready to see if the local news has a report on how widespread the outages are."

As they watched the news, they learned that Royal and the surrounding area had been virtually shut down by the ice storm. There were only a few pockets of people who still had electricity, but as the ice brought down more trees and power lines, the utility company expected those to be without power by morning.

When the news program ended, Kiley got up and walked over to him and Emmie. "She's asleep."

"Do you want me to carry her to bed for you?" he asked, careful to keep his voice low.

She shook her head. "It might frighten her if she wakes up by herself in a strange place." She lifted her daughter to her shoulder. "I'll just lay her down on the love seat until I go to bed."

After laying Emmie on the love seat, Kiley started to sit back down in the armchair, but he caught her hand in his. "Sit here."

"Josh, I'm not overly comfortable—"

"It will be easier to talk without disturbing Emmie," he reasoned, interrupting her.

She stared at him for several long seconds before she slowly lowered herself to the cushion. "I suppose you're right. She normally isn't a light sleeper, but that's at home in her own bed."

"I've been thinking about the sleeping arrangements," he said, nodding.

"And just what about them?" she demanded, looking suspicious.

He couldn't keep from chuckling. "Calm down. There are two master suites—the one down here that you used to give Emmie a bath, and one upstairs. There are also four more bedrooms upstairs. I thought you could take your pick of where you and Emmie are going to sleep. But common sense tells me that little kids and stairs aren't always a good mix."

"Oh." She paused for a moment. "Thank you. That's very considerate. But since your things are in the master suite down here, I assume it's your room?"

He nodded. "Martha has a bad knee and it's easier for her to clean and make the bed if she doesn't have to go up and down the stairs all the time."

Her slow smile sent heat straight to the pit of his belly. "You're one surprise after another, Josh Gordon."

He frowned. "Why do you say that?"

"Not everyone would be that considerate of their housekeeper," she answered.

"I've known Martha and Bobby Ray all my life," he said, shrugging. "When they had to sell off their herds because of the drought, they were in danger of losing their ranch. I offered them jobs because I knew they wouldn't accept help otherwise."

"I can understand that. It's a matter of pride." She seemed to visibly relax as they continued to talk. "Were they able to keep their land?"

He nodded. "They didn't have the money to start over, but since the ranch has been in Bobby Ray's family for over five generations, they wanted to keep it for their grandson. By working for me, they have enough money for their needs, as well as being able to keep the ranch."

"And you make adjustments in your life, so they're able to continue doing that," she said softly.

"Something like that," he answered, feeling a little uncomfortable. He hadn't thought about it as anything more than what it was—the right thing to do.

Deciding it was time to change the focus of their conversation, he grinned. "You know what we need to do tomorrow?"

"I can't imagine," she said, giving him the smile that never failed to send his hormones racing.

"We need to decorate this place for Christmas." He pointed to the corner beside the stone fireplace. "That's where I put the tree the first holiday after I moved in."

"You haven't decorated since then?" she asked, frowning.

"I haven't really had the time." He had, but he hadn't seen any reason to decorate since he was the only one around to appreciate it. "Do you think the tree should go there or somewhere else?"

"By the fireplace is fine," Kiley agreed, hiding a yawn behind her delicate hand. "Emmie and I put ours up on Sunday afternoon. She's going to love getting to decorate another one. But where are you going to get one in this weather?"

"I have a seven-foot artificial tree stored in the garage. But we can talk more about it tomorrow. You're tired," he said, rising to his feet. Holding out his hand to help her up from the couch, he pulled her into his arms. "I'm going to give you a good-night kiss, Kiley." When she started to protest, he put his index finger to her lips. "Just a kiss. Then I'm going to go upstairs—"

"We can sleep—"

He reached up to lightly run the pad of his thumb over her full lower lip, interrupting her protest. "It's all right. I'll take the suite upstairs."

He felt a slight tremor course through her at his touch and without hesitation brought his mouth down to replace his thumb. Careful to keep the kiss non-threatening, Josh barely brushed her lips with his as he waited for an indication from Kiley that she wanted him to take the caress to the next level. When she slowly raised her arms to his shoulders and leaned into him, he felt a moment of triumph. She wanted more, but teasing her with a featherlight touch, he continued to wait. He wanted an indication of her eagerness for his kiss, wanted to know she was impatient for him to give her the kiss she deserved.

Nibbling at her perfect mouth, Josh sensed her increased frustration when a tiny moan escaped her slightly parted lips and she pressed herself closer. "Do you want me to kiss you, Kiley?"

"I...shouldn't," she said, sounding delightfully breathless.

He leaned back to look down at her. "But you do."

"Yes."

It was all he needed to hear, and lowering his head, he covered her mouth with his to give them both what they wanted. Soft and yielding, Kiley had the sweetest lips. Coaxing her to open for him, he deepened the kiss, sending a shaft of heat straight to the region south of his belt buckle.

When she sagged against him, Josh caught her to him. He had no idea why, but even with several inches' difference in their heights, no other woman had ever felt as perfect in his arms as Kiley did. Thinking about how flawlessly they fit together reminded him of that night three years ago and caused his body to harden with need so fast it left him feeling light-headed.

Pulling her more fully against him, he knew the moment Kiley felt his arousal pressed firmly to her. Her breathing quickened and instead of pulling away as he thought she might, she tightened her arms around his shoulders and seemed to melt into him.

The knowledge that she wanted him as much as he wanted her sent his blood pressure sky-high and he sensed that it wouldn't take much for either of them to throw caution to the wind and give in to the explosive chemistry between them. But that wasn't what Josh wanted. When they made love that night in her sister's apartment, their coming together had been frenzied and desperate. And they had both thought they were making love with someone else.

When they made love again—and there wasn't a doubt in his mind that was exactly what was going to eventually happen—he wanted them to take their time. He wanted them to explore each other thoroughly and completely until there was no doubt in either of their minds whom they were making love with.

Slowly easing away from the kiss, Josh took a deep breath. Looking down into her pretty brown eyes still glazed with desire, it was all he could do to keep from resuming the kiss and letting the chips fall where they may.

"J-Josh, I—"

"Shh, honey," he interrupted, kissing the tip of her nose. He released her to walk over to the love seat and pick up her daughter. "Let's get you and Emmie settled in my bedroom. Then I'm going to go upstairs and take a shower cold enough to freeze the balls off a pool table."

Six

The following afternoon, Kiley sat on the couch watching as Josh let Emmie help him put a seven-foot artificial tree together in the corner by the fireplace. It was taking twice as long as it should to assemble the tree because of his "helper." But he didn't seem to mind and patiently waited for her daughter to bring him each branch from the piles he had sorted by length earlier that morning.

Yawning, Kiley laid her head back against the back of the couch. She was completely exhausted and it wasn't hard to figure out why. The kiss they'd shared last night had made her feel as if she would go into total meltdown, and if that hadn't been enough to keep her eyes wide open the entire night, Josh's insistence that she and Emmie sleep in his room was.

The entire suite had that clean, masculine scent

she'd come to associate with him, but when she'd crawled under the covers of his king-size bed, she'd had the sense of being surrounded by him. That had triggered memories of the night he had accidently made love to her, and an accompanying restlessness stronger than anything she could have ever imagined kept her tossing and turning the rest of the night.

"Mommy, see," Emmie said, climbing up on the couch beside her.

Opening her eyes, Kiley smiled at her beautiful little girl. "What do you want me to see, sweetie?"

Emmie beamed as she pointed to the corner by the fireplace. "Twee."

"It's beautiful," Kiley said as she watched Josh plug in the multicolored lights. "You did a really good job helping put it together."

When the tree's branches seemed to instantly come alive with hundreds of twinkling stars, Emmie's eyes widened and she clapped her little hands. "Pwetty."

"It does look pretty good, doesn't it?" Josh grinned. "Would you like to put the angel on the top, Emmie?"

Nodding, Emmie scrambled down from the couch to hurry over to him. As they searched the boxes of ornaments for the tree topper, Kiley couldn't help but notice once again the similarities between them. She had already noticed they had the same eyes and nose, but she now realized that Emmie's hair was closer to Josh's light brown shade than her own dark blonde.

As she watched, Josh lifted Emmie to place the angel on the top of the tree. When they turned to get her opinion, Kiley sucked in a sharp breath. Even their smiles were the same.

She still intended to go through the motion of calling Mark to ask about his blood type, but there was no longer any doubt who had fathered her precious little girl. Emmie looked just like Josh. Confirming the fact was just a matter of formality.

"How does it look?" Josh asked.

"Other than being a bit crooked, it looks fine," she answered automatically.

Setting Emmie on her feet, he walked over to stand in front of her. "Are you feeling all right?"

"Y-yes. Why do you ask?"

"You just looked so—" he paused as if searching for the right word "—preoccupied."

Shaking her head, she forced a smile. "I'm just a little tired. That's all."

He stared at her for several long seconds before nodding. "I didn't sleep all that well myself." He smiled. "I couldn't seem to stop thinking about that kiss and—"

"I didn't say I wasn't able to sleep last night," she interrupted, reluctant to admit to him that she had suffered the same problem.

"You didn't have to, honey," he said, reaching out to tenderly caress her cheek with his calloused palm. "The dark circles under your eyes told me that much."

She wasn't sure she liked Josh's knowing that he had been the reason for her exhaustion. Thinking quickly, she grasped the first excuse that came to mind. "Children tend to be restless sleepers."

Josh stared at her a moment longer. "If you say so," he finally said, turning back toward the boxes of ornaments. She could tell he didn't believe her for a minute, but at least he hadn't pressed the issue.

By the time they finished decorating the tree, Emmie had started rubbing her eyes sleepily and

Kiley knew it was time for her daughter to take a nap. "Emmie, would you like for me to read one of your books to you?"

"Ponies," Emmie said, reaching into Kiley's tote bag.

While she read her daughter's favorite book, Kiley noticed that Josh collected the empty ornament boxes, then, setting one aside, took the others back out to the storage area of the garage. When he came back in, he sat down in the armchair next to the couch. Every time she glanced up, he was staring at her, and she wondered what was running through his mind.

"She's asleep," he finally said, getting up to walk over and lift her daughter from Kiley's lap. Carrying her over to the love seat, she watched him cover Emmie with a colorful Native American blanket. "Would you like a cup of coffee? I made a fresh pot while you were reading to the pony princess," he said, chuckling.

"A cup of coffee sounds wonderful." Maybe the caffeine would help chase away some of her fatigue. "How do you take yours?" she asked, rising to her feet.

"I'll get it." He grinned. "You cooked dinner yesterday evening and, unless a tropical heat wave sweeps through the area to melt all this ice off the roads, you'll probably be cooking again this evening and maybe tomorrow evening. The least I can do is bring you a cup of coffee."

Telling him how she liked her coffee, Kiley sat back down on the couch. For the past few years she had thought of him as a man who couldn't be trusted—an unfeeling jerk who had broken her sister's heart. And in the past several months, she'd come to think of him as the uncaring chairman of the TCC funding committee who, along with some of his fellow committee members, wanted nothing more than to see the day care center fail and her be out of a job.

But the more she got to know him, the more she had to admit that Josh was different than she had perceived him to be. Even before her sister finally confessed that their breakup hadn't gone quite the way she'd told everyone, Kiley had started to realize that he wasn't such a bad guy after all.

If he was as heartless as she'd first thought, he wouldn't have given her a month's worth of the extra money she had asked for and the chance to prove to him that it was needed for the day care center. Nor would he have been concerned for her and Emmie's safety and insisted on driving them to his ranch, rather than her trying to get them home on a treacherous, ice-glazed road.

"Here you go." Laughing, Josh handed her a steaming mug. "Coffee-flavored milk with a little sweetener."

She smiled. "I suppose you're one of the coffee purists?"

He nodded as he sat down beside her. "I like it black, and the stronger the better."

"Aside from the taste, if I drank it like that, I'd never go to sleep." She set her cup on a coaster on the end table. "I didn't even start drinking coffee until after I had Emmie. It was the only way I could stay awake during the day after staying up all night with a colicky baby."

"So when you told me that your ex-husband left

right after Emmie was born, you meant immediately after?" he asked, frowning.

"Mark moved out four days after she was born." Kiley shrugged. "Looking back on it, I'm just as glad that he did. Taking care of a baby was enough to keep me busy. I didn't need a demanding, immature male to deal with at the same time."

"What about your mom or your sister?" Josh asked, sounding genuinely interested. "Surely they helped out."

She nodded. "They were there for me as much as they could be. But they both had to work. Besides, Emmie was my baby to take care of."

He seemed to think over what she had just told him before he finally nodded. "I can understand your sense of responsibility, but it couldn't have been easy. What about some time for yourself?"

"If by that you're asking if I've seen anyone since she was born, the answer is no." She smiled lovingly at her little girl sleeping so peacefully on the love seat. "It might have been extremely difficult at times, but there isn't a single second of it that I regret. I don't need a social life—I have my daughter. Nothing is more important to me than being her mother."

Setting his coffee on the end table, Josh moved closer to her. "You're a great mom and Emmie is a great kid," he said, pulling her into his arms.

"Josh, what are you doing?" she asked, wishing her tone had been a bit more demanding.

"I'm trying to remind you that besides being a great mom, you're a beautiful, desirable woman." He brushed her mouth with his. "You want to know what I think?"

"Probably not," she said, wondering why she couldn't be more assertive. All he had to do was take her into his arms and she seemed to lose every ounce of common sense she'd ever possessed.

He rested his forehead against hers. "I think you need to hear that on a regular basis." Kissing his way down her cheek, she could feel his smile against her skin. "I know you'd rather not think about it, but I know firsthand just how passionate and desirable you are."

A shiver of awareness streaked up her spine and for the first time in years, she was keenly aware of how long it had been since she'd felt anything even close to passion and desire. "You're right," she said, meaning it. "I'd rather not think about that night."

"But it's something neither of us will ever forget, honey." He kissed his way down the side of her neck. "I know every time I look at you, it's just about all I'm able to think about," he admitted as he nibbled at the rapidly beating pulse at the base of her throat. "We might have made love by mistake, but I can't say I'm sorry about it."

"I—I…thought you…were Mark," she said defensively.

"And I thought you were Lori." He cupped her cheeks with his hands and lifted her gaze to meet his. "But that doesn't negate the fact that something happened between us that night that was nothing short of amazing."

As she stared into his remarkable blue eyes, Kiley knew what he said was true. She had never felt anything even close to the connection, the intimacy she had experienced with Josh. It was as if their souls had touched.

"You felt it, too," he stated. It wasn't a question, and she knew by the look on his handsome face that it would be futile to deny it.

Instead of waiting for her response, he lowered his head. The moment their lips met, Kiley felt as if stars burst behind her closed eyes and it seemed that time came to a halt. The awareness she felt whenever she was around him became a magnetic pull that she found impossible to resist, and she couldn't have kept herself from melting against him if her life depended on it.

When he traced her lips with his tongue, she automatically parted them on a soft sigh, inviting him to deepen the caress. As he tenderly stroked her inner recesses, Kiley marveled at how exciting and arousing it was each time he kissed her. Josh Gordon was an expert, and there wasn't a doubt in her mind that he could seduce a marble statue with nothing more than his talented mouth.

Sliding his hand from her back along her side, when he cupped her breast and teased the puckered tip with the pad of his thumb, Kiley thought she would be swamped by the seemingly endless waves of heat sweeping over her. The sensations were so exquisite, she felt branded by his gentle touch.

"Kiley…honey, there's something…going on between us," he said, sounding as out of breath as she felt. "It started that night in your sister's apartment… and it's just as strong now, if not stronger, than it was then." He gave her a kiss so tender it brought tears to her eyes. "All I'm asking is that you acknowledge that."

She couldn't deny that there was something drawing them together much like a bee was drawn to a field of wildflowers. But she wasn't altogether sure she was ready to admit it either.

"We do seem to share an awareness of sorts," she said, choosing her words carefully. She tried to be honest without revealing the full impact of his effect on her.

To her surprise, instead of arguing with her to try to get her to admit that it was more than a mild attraction between them, Josh kissed her soundly, then, releasing her, stood up. "That's all I needed to hear." He took her hand in his and, pulling her to her feet, handed her the box he had set aside earlier. "Could you do me a favor and decorate the mantel, while I take care of hanging a few lights around the front door?"

Relieved and much more comfortable with his shift of focus, she nodded. "After I finish, I'll start dinner."

"Sounds like a plan," he said, giving her a lingering kiss that caused her toes to curl into the plush carpet.

As she watched him turn and stroll down the hall toward the front door, she sighed. How could life become so complicated in such a short span of time?

Opening the box he'd handed her, she placed holly and pinecones along the top of the mantel. It had been so much easier to think of Josh as the heartbreaking Ebenezer Scrooge of the TCC funding committee. She almost wished that she still could. It would be a lot less stressful than the reality of the kind, thoughtful man that he had turned out to be.

On Wednesday afternoon, Josh stood in his family room, staring at the Christmas tree he and Emmie had put up the day before. When had his house become so damned big and empty? He had lived in the place for over five years and in all that time, he couldn't think of a single time that he had felt as alone as he did at that moment.

After the morning news reported that the roads were clear and that power had been restored to the subdivision where Kiley lived, they'd gone to the TCC clubhouse to get Kiley's car, then he'd come home to work. But he hadn't expected to find himself listening for Kiley as she moved around in the kitchen cooking or the sound of Emmie's delightful giggles as she played with her toy ponies.

"You're losing it, Gordon," he muttered as he walked down the hall to his office.

He liked being a bachelor—liked living alone. He could do what he wanted, when he wanted, and there wasn't anyone but himself to worry about. Besides, he had work to do and didn't have time for anything else.

An hour later, he uttered a heartfelt curse and turned off his computer. He had been working on the same bid sheet since he'd sat down and gotten absolutely nowhere with it. All he had been able to do was sit there wondering what Kiley and Emmie were doing.

Had the house been warm enough when they arrived home? Did she need him to check out the plumbing to make sure the water pipes hadn't frozen from the low temperatures and caused a leak? What were they planning to have for dinner? Did they miss having him around?

Rising from his desk chair, he walked out of his office and straight through the house to the door leading to the garage. He grabbed a jacket on the way through the mudroom and within minutes, Josh was driving down the highway toward Royal.

By the time he knocked on Kiley's door, he was confident his plans for the evening were set. He would see if she needed anything, then he fully intended to pick up takeout at his favorite Chinese restaurant, go back home and work on the bid sheet he needed to turn in for the new addition to the women's crisis center over in Somerset.

"Josh, I didn't expect to see you again until Monday afternoon," Kiley said, looking confused when she let him in. "Is something wrong?"

"No, I just wanted to check in and make sure you and Emmie made it home all right." He realized how lame his excuse sounded. Picking up the phone and giving her a call would have accomplished the same thing.

"Hi," Emmie said, grinning as she ran up to him and held up her arms.

"Hi," he said, picking her up. "How's the pony princess?"

She surprised him when she put her little arms around his neck to give him a big hug, then started jabbering excitedly. He looked to Kiley for a translation.

"Emmie thinks you're here for dinner and a movie," Kiley said, smiling. "She wants you to stay."

"And what does her mom want?" he asked, lightly running his index finger along her smooth cheek.

As she stared up at him, he felt her turn ever so slightly into his touch. It was almost imperceptible, but there was no denying it had happened.

"I was going to pick up Chinese on the way home,"

he said, trailing his finger over her lower lip. "Why
don't we have it delivered here?"

"Okay," she said, suddenly taking her daughter
from him and backing away. "I'll give Emmie a bath
and get her ready for bed. That way she can go to sleep
while we watch the movie."

He had a good idea why she had retreated. Unless he missed his guess, she was frightened by the
strength of the chemistry between them. Hell, it was
pretty unsettling for him as well. But he knew beyond
a shadow of doubt that if they didn't explore it further,
he would end up regretting it for the rest of his life. He
had a feeling she would, too.

Two hours later, Josh couldn't help but smile as
he sat on Kiley's couch, waiting for her to finish getting Emmie tucked in for the night. They had stuffed
themselves on lo mein and egg rolls, then watched the
movie about the little mermaid princess again. And
if anyone had told him a week ago that he would be
happy staying in, watching a kids' cartoon for the second time in less than a week, he would have told them
they were in serious need of psychiatric evaluation.

It wasn't that he was a player or ever had been.
But his idea of a good time had always been taking a
woman to dinner, maybe a little dancing afterward,
and seeing where the evening led them.

He suddenly sat up straight as the realization set in
that he hadn't even asked Kiley out on a date. They had
spent a week and a half seeing each other as often as
he could arrange, shared some extremely passionate
kisses and, even though it had been three years ago and
due to a case of mistaken identity, they had made love.
But he hadn't taken her out for a night on the town.

Deciding to remedy that oversight, he waited for her to walk back into her living room. "Kiley, come over here and sit down. I have something I need to ask you."

"What would that be?" she asked, looking as if she dreaded what he might want to know.

When she sank down on the cushion beside him, he put his arms around her. "I know this is short notice, but would you be my date for the TCC's Christmas Ball on Saturday night?"

"That's all?" she asked, visibly relaxing.

Nodding, Josh frowned. "What did you think I wanted to ask you?"

She stared at him for a moment before she finally shook her head and smiled. "I...wasn't sure."

Pulling her closer, he lowered his mouth to hers to nibble and nip at her lower lip. "As much as I enjoy spending time with Emmie watching the mermaid cartoon, I'd like to take her mother out for dinner and an evening of dancing."

He felt a shiver course through her. "Josh, I don't usually...go out."

"How long has it been since you went dancing?" he asked, kissing his way to the slight hollow at the base of her throat.

"I...uh...before Emmie was born," she said, sounding distracted.

"You're joking." He leaned back to look at her. "You haven't gone out since your divorce?"

"No."

"Surely you've enjoyed an evening with some of your friends," he said, having a hard time believing that she hadn't at least had a girls' night out.

She shook her head. "All of my friends are married

and most of them have children. We're all too busy. Besides, going to clubs is expensive."

He pulled her back against his chest for a comforting hug. She had just confirmed his suspicion that she struggled to make ends meet, and he suddenly wanted to find her ex-husband and give him a lesson in facing up to his responsibilities that the man wouldn't soon forget.

"Having kids doesn't mean you can't get out and socialize." He kissed her forehead. "I'm not an expert by any means, but I think interaction with other adults would be a necessity after dealing with kids all the time."

"I didn't say I don't spend time with my friends," she said, defensively. "We sometimes get together on Saturday afternoons for shopping trips to the mall. And tomorrow I'm going to lunch with Piper Kindred."

"I think that's great, honey." He cupped her cheek with his palm and, staring into her warm brown eyes, he smiled. "But I want to take you out on a date. I want to hold you in my arms when we dance and remind you of what a beautiful, desirable woman you are."

"I'd have to find a dress and arrange for someone to watch Emmie," she said, her tone uncertain. "And I'm not sure that it isn't frowned on for employees of the Texas Cattleman's Club to attend special events like the Christmas Ball."

Frowning, Josh shook his head. "Let's clear up something right now. Members of the TCC might be affluent, but we aren't snobs. I can't think of anyone who would have a problem with you being my date for the evening."

"Not even Beau Hacket or Paul Windsor?" she

asked, arching one perfect eyebrow. "I'm sure one of them would have something to say."

"Beau Hacket will be too busy bragging about his son Hack's latest accomplishments to think of anything else. And the biggest issue with Paul Windsor would be him trying to put the moves on you." Grinning, he shook his head. "That's an opportunity I don't intend to give Windsor or anyone else."

"I don't know, Josh. It's been so long since—"

"Just say yes, Kiley."

"I probably wouldn't be able to get a sitter on such short notice," she hedged.

He pulled his cell phone from his shirt pocket and handed it to her. "Call your parents and see if they can keep Emmie for the night."

"Why?"

"It's going to be late by the time we leave the ball, then we would have to drive the fifty miles up to Midland and back to get her," he answered. "I just figured you might not want to disturb her sleep."

Kiley stared at him for several seconds before she nodded and handed his phone back to him. "I'll use the phone in my office."

While she went to make the call to ask her parents about keeping Emmie Saturday evening, Josh thought of something else he needed to do. Kiley had mentioned she would need to find a dress for the ball, and he could imagine just what a dent the price of an evening gown would make in her budget. If she'd let him, he would like nothing more than to make things easier for her by giving her one of his credit cards to use. But if there was one thing he had learned in the past week and a half, it was how fiercely independent she was. She would no doubt tell him where he could put his card, as well as tell him to find someone else to go to the ball with him.

Deciding that he could use a little assistance with his idea, he made a mental note to call Piper Kindred first thing tomorrow. He had heard that she and Kiley had become friends when Piper taught a CPR class at the TCC clubhouse, and he had known Piper for years. He knew he could count on her to help him out.

"What did they say?" he asked when Kiley walked back into the living room.

"They're thrilled that I'm going to the ball," she said, frowning as she sat back down on the couch beside him. "My mother even told me it's past time that I started dating again."

"Your mom sounds like a wise woman," he said, pulling Kiley to him. He was a bit surprised that her mother approved of Kiley going to the ball with him, considering the story Lori had planned on telling them after they broke up. Either Kiley's mother had forgotten who he was or, at some point in the past three years, Lori had come clean and told them the truth about how their brief relationship had ended.

Deciding it didn't matter, he gave Kiley a kiss that sent his blood pressure sky-high and caused his jeans to feel as if they were a few sizes too small. "I'm sure she just wants you to be happy."

"I know, but I'm so…out of practice at the whole dating thing," she said, shrugging one slender shoulder.

"The ball may be our first date, but it's not like we haven't spent a lot of time together in the past couple of weeks," he said, kissing her temple. "And let me assure you that I plan on spending a lot more with you in the future."

"Josh, I have Emmie...to think about." She melted against him. "I have to think of what's best for her."

He knew Kiley's reluctance stemmed from her concern that Emmie might become too attached to him and end up being hurt, not to mention the possibility of being rejected herself. The way that bastard of an ex-husband had walked out on her and Emmie, it was no wonder she was afraid of taking a chance on another relationship.

His heart came to a screeching halt and he had to take a deep breath. What the hell was he thinking? He wasn't looking for anything long-term, was he?

It was true that he had been relentless in getting close to Kiley because he wanted her to admit there was an overwhelming chemistry between them. And she had done that. But beyond that, he hadn't given it much thought. Did he want to try exploring something exclusive with her?

He wasn't sure. But he was certain of one thing. Just the thought of anyone, himself included, causing her or Emmie any kind of distress was more than he could tolerate. Nor could he stand the thought of Kiley in the arms of another man.

"Honey, I give you my word that I will gladly walk through hell and back before I hurt you or Emmie in any way," he assured her.

Needing to make sure she understood that he meant every word he said, Josh lowered his mouth to hers. For reasons he didn't care to analyze too closely, all he wanted to do was make Kiley happy, to show her how special she was to him and to make things easier for her and her delightful little girl.

When Kiley placed her hand over his heart, the warmth of her palm and the feel of her caressing his chest through the fabric of his chambray shirt set off little electric charges throughout his being. Heat rushed through his veins and his body hardened with an urgency that left him feeling light-headed.

At that moment, nothing would have pleased him more than to remove both of their clothes and make love to her right there on her couch. But Kiley wasn't ready and he didn't care how many cold showers he had to endure, he wasn't going to rush her. When they made love again, it would be because it was what they both wanted, what they could no longer resist.

"I think I'd better leave," he said, breaking the kiss.

As he gazed down at her, he came close to losing his resolve. The passion and desire in her luminous brown eyes was breathtaking and he knew as surely as he knew his own name, they would be making love soon.

"If you and Emmie need anything, don't hesitate to let me know," he said, standing up. He took her hand to help her to her feet, then led her over to the door. Brushing her perfect lips with his, he smiled. "I'll see you when I drop by the day care center on Friday afternoon, Kiley."

Seven

The following day, when Kiley parked her car outside the Royal Diner, she checked the time on her cell phone. She was running a little late and she hoped that Piper had already found them a booth.

"Over here, Kiley," Piper called to her.

Spotting her friend, Kiley smiled and made her way toward the back of the newly renovated diner. A paramedic working out of Royal Memorial Hospital, Piper had been the instructor for the first-aid and CPR classes Kiley had arranged for the TCC employees. She had wanted to make sure that in case of an emergency with the children at the day care center, everyone knew exactly what to do and how to administer aid if it was needed.

"Sorry I'm late," she said, sliding into the booth on the opposite side of the table from her friend. "I had to wait for one of my volunteers to arrive to help Carrie with the children's afternoon activities."

Piper shook her head. "Don't worry about it. I just got here myself."

"So what's up?" Kiley asked, picking up the plastic-covered menu. "When you called the other day you sounded a little panicked."

"I need your help," Piper said, looking a bit uncomfortable. "I know I've probably put it off way too long, but I need a dress for the Christmas Ball and we both know I'm a lot more comfortable in jeans and a flannel shirt than I am in an evening gown." She grinned. "I was hoping you'd go with me this afternoon to help pick it out."

"Of course I'll go with you," Kiley answered, relieved that nothing was seriously wrong. "In fact, I was going to look for a dress for the ball myself this afternoon. Josh Gordon asked me to be his date."

Piper grinned. "Keep your friends close and your enemies closer?"

Kiley grinned sheepishly. "Something like that."

"I knew there had to be something going on between the two of you," Piper said, nodding. "Your reaction to him a few weeks back was just a little too strong for there not to be."

"Well, at that time I thought he was about as trustworthy as a snake," she said, laughing. "But I've recently discovered that he isn't all that bad." Even her parents had revised their opinion of Josh and didn't seem to question her decision to start seeing him after her sister confessed her role in their breakup three years ago.

"Josh is a really nice guy," Piper agreed. "In fact,

most of the members of the TCC are basically good guys. Some of them might have a few rough edges, but they really do try to live by the TCC code."

As they continued to chat about who they thought would be attending the ball and the type of dresses they wanted to look for, Kiley noticed a woman with dark brown hair sitting at a table close by. She had finished her lunch, but seemed to be taking great interest in what they had to say. So much so that Kiley could tell she was delaying her departure. Only when the conversation turned to the shopping trip they were planning to find dresses for the event did the woman get up to go pay her bill and leave.

"Did you notice that woman eavesdropping?" Piper asked as they watched her walk up to the counter to pay for her meal.

Kiley nodded. "I wonder who she is."

"I don't know, but I intend to find out," Piper said, motioning for Amanda Battle, the manager of the diner, to come over to their booth.

"How can I help you two?" Amanda asked, smiling.

"Who was that woman sitting at the table next to us?" Piper asked, cutting right to the heart of the matter.

Amanda glanced toward the front of the diner where the woman was just leaving. "That was Britt Collins, the detective in charge of investigating Alex Santiago's kidnapping."

"That explains why she was so interested when we started talking about the TCC," Kiley commented.

Suddenly distracted by the tall, dark-haired man entering the diner, Kiley placed her napkin on the table. She had tried to phone her ex-husband the day before to inquire about his blood type, but he hadn't returned her call. She wasn't going to let him get away without answering her question now.

"If you two will excuse me, I see someone I need to talk to," she said. "I'll be right back."

Walking over to his table, Kiley wasn't surprised when he looked around as if trying to find a way to escape.

"What do you want?" he asked, clearly unhappy about seeing her again. "I figured when I didn't call you back yesterday that you'd get the idea that I don't want to have anything to do with you or the brat."

"You couldn't possibly want to avoid having to talk to me as much as I want to avoid talking to you," Kiley said, wondering what she'd ever seen in the man. "I only called yesterday because I need to know your blood type."

"What do you need that for?" he demanded as if she'd asked him to reveal some deep, dark secret.

"It's for Emmie's medical records," she said, thinking quickly.

"Is that it?" he asked, looking suspicious.

"That's it," she assured him. When he told her his blood type, she nodded. "Thank you."

Without another word, she turned to walk back to the booth where Piper still sat talking to Amanda. Kiley had known in her heart that her suspicions were well-founded, but to have them confirmed was almost more than she could come to terms with.

She had done enough research on blood types and establishing paternity by that method to know that for the past three years the man she had thought to be Emmie's father, wasn't. Now all she had to do was find the right time and way to tell Josh Gordon that the little girl he fondly called the "pony princess" was his daughter.

Driving across Royal, Josh went through four traffic lights on yellow and, looking both ways, rolled through two stop signs as he sped toward Kiley's. When she'd called, she wouldn't tell him what was wrong, only that it was urgent that she see him right away.

When he finally pulled into her driveway, he barely had the engine turned off before he was out of the car and sprinting his way up to her door. Not bothering to knock before he entered the house, he stopped short when he spotted Kiley sitting in the armchair beside the couch, glaring at him.

"Are you and Emmie all right?"

"We're just fine," she answered. "But you're not."

A strong sense of relief washed over him. She was upset, but otherwise, she and Emmie were okay. "So what's wrong?"

"You know what's wrong," she accused, her brown eyes sparkling with anger. "How dare you?"

"How dare I what?" He feigned ignorance, but he had a good idea why she was in a snit.

"You used my friendship with Piper to steer me to the dress shop where you had made arrangements to pay for my dress," she accused.

He glanced at the garment bag from one of Royal's exclusive boutiques draped over the back of the couch. He'd figured she wouldn't be overly happy with him, but he hadn't counted on her being downright furious that he had arranged to buy the dress she would be wearing to the Christmas Ball.

Slowly closing the door, he looked around as he walked farther into the living room. "Have you already got Emmie in bed for the night?"

"Yes. Why?"

He nodded. "That's good. I'd hate for her to have to listen to us argue. It might upset her."

"There isn't going to be an argument," Kiley insisted. "You're going to take your dress and leave."

"Sorry, honey, you're going to have to keep it," he said, grinning. "It isn't my size." He knew immediately that a flippant remark was the wrong thing to say.

Her eyes narrowed and her cheeks turned crimson as her obvious anger rose. "You bought it. You can keep it, take it back or stick it where the sun never shines." She shook her head. "It really doesn't matter to me. Just take it and go."

"Now, honey—"

"Don't you 'now, honey' me, Josh Gordon." She stood up and came to stand in front of him. "Let's get something straight right now," she said, poking him in the chest with her index finger. "I'm not a charity case. I pay my own way."

After her reaction to his glib comment, he knew better than to grin. But damn she was cute when she was all fired up about something.

"I understand that you want to be independent and I respect that, Kiley," he said, reaching out to put his arms around her. When she tried to push herself free, he tightened his arms and pulled her more fully against him. "But I also know an evening gown wasn't something you planned to buy." He brought his hand up to lift her chin until their gazes met. "I asked you to go with me to the ball because I wanted you to have a good time, not to wreck your budget."

"I could have charged it," she insisted.

"I know that," he said, nodding. "But the point I'm trying to make is this—when I take a woman out for the evening, I want her to relax and enjoy herself. I don't want her having to worry about how she's going to pay for the dress she's wearing."

Before she could argue with him further, Josh lowered his mouth to hers. Unyielding at first, he moved his lips over hers until she melted against him. Then, using his tongue, he sought entry to lightly stroke and tease her inner recesses. No other woman had ever tasted sweeter and he knew without question that if he wasn't already, he could quickly become addicted to kissing her.

Bringing his hand up under the hem of her sweatshirt, he released the front clasp of her bra to cup her breast with his palm. Caressing the soft, full mound, he grazed the beaded tip with the pad of his thumb, causing a tiny moan to escape her parted lips. His body responded instantly and he didn't think twice about pressing himself to her. He wanted her to feel what she did to him, how she made him want her.

As he eased away from the kiss, he stared down into her passion-glazed brown eyes. "I'm still angry with you," she said stubbornly.

"I know, honey." Nodding, he removed his hand from her shirt. "But please believe me when I tell you it was never my intention to upset you. All I wanted to do was make it easier on you." He kissed her until they both gasped for breath. "Now, I'm going to go back home because if I don't, I'm going to take you into the bedroom and spend the rest of the night making love to you."

She worried her lower lip for a moment before she spoke. "Josh, we need to talk."

"Is it something that can wait?" he asked, knowing that if he didn't put distance between them, and damned quick, he wouldn't have the strength to leave.

"I suppose so," she said, nodding.

"Good." He pressed his lips to hers for a quick kiss, then, setting her away from him, walked to the door. "Because right now, I have to get back to my place. I have an ice-cold shower waiting on me and a sleepless night ahead." He laughed in an attempt to release some of the tension gripping him. "I think it's about time for me to get started on it."

As Kiley watched Josh close the door behind him, she caught her lower lip between her teeth. She had started to tell him that Emmie was his daughter. But when he stopped her, she had readily gone along with putting off the inevitable for just a bit longer. She couldn't decide if she was being a coward for not insisting that he listen to her, or just being cautious.

For one thing, she wasn't quite sure how to start the conversation, nor was she looking forward to his reaction to the news. There was no doubt he would be shocked. But there was also the possibility that he would think she was trying to use her daughter to sway his recommendation to the funding committee. He knew how important her job was to her and how much it meant to be able to be with Emmie while she still made a living to support them.

Unfortunately, time was not on her side. The more

he was around Emmie the greater the chance he would realize she not only looked like him, the timeline for her birth supported that he had fathered her.

Kiley took a deep breath as she reached for the garment bag with her new evening gown and walked down the hall to hang it in her closet. The funding committee would be meeting next week and unless something happened to further complicate the matter or the perfect opportunity presented itself, she might do well to wait until the day care center's fate had been decided.

Then she had every intention of making him listen to her whether he wanted to hear what she had to say or not.

On Saturday evening when Kiley opened the door, her breath caught. Josh looked utterly devastating in his tailored black tuxedo. But it was the look of appreciation in his blue eyes that caused her heart to skip several beats.

"You look so beautiful, Kiley." He stepped just inside the door to take her in his arms and give her a soft, lingering kiss. "I'll be the envy of every man at the ball."

"I was just thinking something very similar about you and the women attending the ball," she said, smiling.

They hadn't seen each other since their argument over the evening gown. He had been busy working up bids for construction jobs, as well as overseeing several Gordon Construction job sites. But that wasn't to say that they hadn't had contact. He'd had flowers delivered to her at the day care center the day before,

and he'd called her last night to ask about her day and
see that she and Emmie were doing all right.

"Is the pony princess okay with staying at your
folks'?" he asked, as he helped her with her evening
wrap.

Nodding, Kiley picked up her sequined clutch. "I
don't know who was more excited about her spending
the night with them, Emmie or my parents. She has
them wrapped around her little finger."

Josh laughed as he placed his hand to her elbow and
guided her out to his car. "She has that effect on just
about everyone. She's an adorable little girl."

"Thank you," Kiley said, hoping she had made the
right decision to wait until after the funding committee meeting to tell him that Emmie was his daughter.

Kiley jumped when Josh kissed her forehead. "I
don't know what's running through that pretty head
of yours," he said, helping her into the passenger seat
of his Mercedes. "But frowning isn't allowed this evening. Only smiles."

As he drove them to the TCC clubhouse for the
club's biggest event of the year, Kiley decided he was
right. Even if she hadn't made the decision to wait to
tell him about Emmie, tonight wasn't a good time.
When they talked, they would need privacy and plenty
of time to sort everything out.

When Josh stopped the car at the front entrance,
he handed his keys to a valet, then came around the
front of the car and opened the passenger door for her.
"This is beautiful, Josh," she said, looking around as
she got out of the car.

The TCC's maintenance crew had strung white
twinkle lights into an arched tunnel over the entrance

for the ball's attendees to walk through. Complemented by big red velvet bows, the effect was magical.

"Haven't you attended one of these in the past?" he asked, tucking her hand into the crook of his arm as they started to walk through the tunnel of lights.

"No, I didn't move to Royal until I graduated from college and Mark wasn't a member of the club," she answered as she looked at all the pretty decorations.

"Wait until you see how they've decorated inside," he said, smiling as the doorman opened the big ornate oak entrance door for them. "The club spares no expense in making this *the* event of the year."

Inside the foyer gorgeous red and white poinsettias had replaced the usual flower arrangements on the hall tables, and big bows adorned the tops of every doorway. "This is absolutely beautiful," she said, taking it all in. "How long will they leave it this way?"

"They'll take everything down the day after New Year's," he said as they walked past several groups of couples greeting each other just outside the Grand Ballroom.

"I'm glad it will be like this the day of the children's Christmas program," she commented. "It will make everything so much more festive."

His smile sent a delicious warmth spreading throughout her body. "What day is the program?"

"This coming Tuesday."

"I'll make sure I'm free," he promised, kissing her temple.

"To check up on the use of the extra funds?" she asked.

"No." He stopped to gaze down at her from his much taller height. "I'll be there because Emmie is in the program and her beautiful mother will be directing it."

His low, intimate tone caused her knees to wobble and a delightful little flutter to stir in the pit of her stomach. But it was the spark of desire she detected in his intense gaze that stole her breath and sent a shiver of need streaking up her spine.

To distract herself from the sudden tension gripping her, she pointed toward a couple standing by the doors to the Grand Ballroom. "There's Piper and her fiancé, Ryan Grant." Concentrating on the emerald-green gown her friend had chosen the day they went shopping, Kiley walked over to hug her. "You look beautiful, Piper. The gown complements your red hair perfectly."

"Thank you." Piper smiled. "I was thinking the same thing about you. I know I told you the other day, but that black dress is gorgeous and looks like it was made just for you."

While Josh and Ryan talked about the new Western wear store Gordon Construction was building, Kiley smiled at Piper. "Are you feeling a little more confident?"

Piper grinned. "If by that you mean, do I still feel like a fish out of water in a dress, the answer is yes." She laughed. "But the look on Ryan's face when he saw me in it for the first time was well worth it."

Kiley knew what her friend meant. The look of appreciation in Josh's eyes had been absolutely breathtaking and she knew for certain it was one she would never forget.

As the conversation wound down, they walked into the ballroom and Kiley continued to marvel at the elaborate decorations. Dark green holly ringed gold-and-silver tapers that served as centerpieces on the round banquet tables, which were covered with pristine white tablecloths. But it was the fifteen-foot Douglas fir Christmas tree in one corner at the front of the room that caused her to catch her breath. It was huge, perfectly shaped and decorated with thousands of blue twinkle lights. A huge silver loopy bow served as a tree topper, its wide ribbon streamers cascading elegantly down over the branches. The effect was stunning.

Kiley enjoyed listening to the conversation at their table throughout dinner. They were seated with Piper and Ryan, Alex Santiago and his fiancée, Cara Windsor, and Josh's twin, Sam, and his wife, Lila. The brothers entertained them all with stories of how they had traded places in a variety of situations and the many pranks they pulled on their friends. And Ryan shared some humorous anecdotes about his days on the rodeo circuit. Alex seemed rather quiet throughout the evening, but that was understandable. He still suffered from amnesia and had no memory of his childhood or past events, but he did seem to enjoy listening to his friends tell about their antics.

Sitting beside her, Piper leaned close. "Are you enjoying yourself?"

"Absolutely," Kiley answered. "I love my daughter more than life itself, but I hadn't realized how much I missed social situations and adult conversation." Smiling, she asked, "How about you? Still feeling like a fish out of water?"

Piper laughed. "I've never been a 'girlie' girl by any

stretch of the imagination, but dressing up and pretending to be one isn't as bad as I thought it would be."

When Ryan claimed Piper's attention, Alex Santiago smiled at her from across the table. "I hear you are doing amazing things at the day care center."

"I'm not sure how amazing it is, but I love what I do," Kiley answered, smiling back. "The children's Christmas program is next week. We'd love to have you join us if you're feeling up to it."

"I think I would like that," Alex said, looking thoughtful.

As Alex turned to greet a fellow TCC member, Josh's twin brother, Sam, spoke up. "In a couple of years we'll be needing the services of the day care center for our twins."

"Even if I decide I'm not going to go back to work, I'll probably need the respite." Lila laughed. "Especially if they're anything like Sam."

When the band started playing, Kiley and Josh sat in companionable silence for a time as they listened to the music. But when the singer introduced a slow song, Josh smiled as he rose to his feet and held out his hand. "Would you like to dance, honey?"

"I haven't danced in so long, I've probably forgotten how," she answered, laughing as she placed her hand in his.

"It's just like riding a bicycle," he said, leading her out onto the dance floor. "Once you learn, you never forget."

As he took her in his arms and placed his hand at her back, Kiley's heart skipped a beat and her knees threatened to give way. The feel of his warm palm caressing the skin exposed by the low-cut back of her gown was intoxicating and caused a longing within her stronger than anything she could have ever imagined.

"We'll have to do this again sometime." He pulled her close to whisper in her ear. "Although I have recently discovered there's a lot to be said for staying in on Saturday nights."

His breath feathering over her ear and the heat from his hand on her back reminded her of just how long it had been since she'd been held by a man as they danced, how much she missed the closeness. She briefly wondered if anyone watched them, but everything around them seemed to fade into nothingness as she stared into Josh's heated gaze.

"Y-You really like eating in front of the television and watching cartoon movies?" she asked, hoping to distract herself from the heat swirling throughout her body.

Shrugging, he smiled. "Watching the show with the pony princess is a lot of fun. But it really starts to get interesting after she's gone to bed and I get to hold and kiss her enticing mother."

The evidence of his rapidly hardening body pressed to her stomach made her feel as if her insides had been turned to warm pudding and she found herself clinging to him for support. "Josh—"

"I'm not going to lie to you, Kiley," he said, his expression turning serious. "I want you and nothing would please me more than to take you home, get you out of this slinky black dress and sink myself so deep inside of you that we both forget where you end and I begin. But that isn't going to happen unless it's what you want, too."

Staring up into his smoldering blue eyes, her heart

began to beat double time and her breathing became shallow. Before they took such an important step, she really needed to tell him about being Emmie's father. "Josh, I…want you, too. But—"

Pressed tightly against her, she felt his body surge at her admission. "There's no 'buts' about it. Do you want me, Kiley?"

"Yes, but we need to talk about something first," she said, wondering why she couldn't sound more insistent.

"Honey, we can talk as much as you want later on," he said, leading her off the dance floor. They stopped by their table for her clutch and evening wrap and came face-to-face with Sam as they turned toward the exit.

"Hey, where are you two going? The night's still young," he said, his eyes twinkling mischievously.

"Can it, bro," Josh said, glaring at his twin.

Seemingly unaffected by his brother's displeasure, Sam turned to her. "It was very nice to meet you, Kiley. If this boneheaded brother of mine gives you any problems, you just let me know."

Kiley smiled and nodded. "I enjoyed meeting you and Lila, as well."

"You and Lila have a nice evening and I'll see you at work on Monday, Sam," Josh said over his shoulder as he hurried her toward the exit. Fortunately the other couples were out on the dance floor and they didn't have to explain their early departure to anyone else.

As they stood beneath the twinkling white lights as they waited for the valet to bring Josh's Mercedes to the front entrance, she felt compelled to try again to tell him about Emmie before things between them went any further. "Josh, please. It's really important that I talk to you about—"

He cut her off with a deep, lingering kiss, then, lightly running his finger along her jaw, he smiled. "I give you my word that we'll discuss whatever is on your mind tomorrow. But tonight is all about us, Kiley. This thing—this need—between us has been building since you walked into the meeting room to address the funding committee, and it's past time we explored it."

Her pulse raced as he helped her into the car, then drove away from the TCC clubhouse. There was no question that the chemistry between them was explosive, but was she ready to take what seemed like the next natural step with Josh? She still hadn't managed to tell him that he was Emmie's real father.

"We aren't going back to my house?" she asked when he steered the Mercedes toward his ranch.

The look he gave her sent heat sweeping throughout her entire body and she forgot anything else she was about to say. "You've slept in my bed without me," he said, his voice low and intimate. "But not tonight." Reaching across the car's console, he took her hand in his and raised it to his mouth to kiss. "Tonight I'm going to hold you and make love to you the way you were meant to be loved. And I'm not about to let anything interrupt that."

The promise in his words and the look on his handsome face caused her to shiver with anticipation, and by the time they reached his ranch, she knew she really didn't have any choice in the matter. Heaven help her, she wanted to once again experience the power of his lovemaking, needed to feel as cherished as when he'd made love to her that night three years ago.

Eight

When they reached his place, Josh led her directly into his bedroom, closed the door and turned on the bedside lamp. Taking her wrap and sequined clutch from her, he placed them on the dresser, then, turning back, he took her in his arms. Any second thoughts she might have had evaporated like the morning mist on a warm summer's day when he lowered his head to capture her lips with his.

His firm mouth moved over hers with an expertise that left her breathless, and she realized that no other man's kiss had ever caused her to react quite the way Josh's did. With sudden clarity, she knew no other man's kiss ever would.

Running his hands along her sides, he nibbled his way down the side of her neck to the base of her throat. "Honey, would you like to know what I've been thinking ever since you opened your door this evening and I saw you in this slinky black dress?"

"I—I'm not sure," she admitted. She shivered with anticipation when he brought his hand up and trailed his index finger along the V neckline of her gown.

"All I've been able to do is think of ways to take it off you," he whispered, kissing her collarbone and the valley between her breasts. "And when we were dancing I wasn't sure I wouldn't lose my mind."

"Wh-why?" She had to concentrate hard to keep from melting into a puddle at his feet.

"When I put my hand to your bare back I couldn't help but imagine how it would feel to caress every inch of your soft skin." There was such passion in his deep baritone, a wave of heat streaked from the top of her head to the soles of her feet.

Her knees threatened to give way and Kiley placed her hands on his chest to steady herself. "I'd like to touch you, too."

The look in his eyes stole her breath a moment before he stepped away from her to remove his tuxedo jacket and tug his shirt from the waistband of his trousers. He held her gaze with his, and neither of them said a word as he unfastened the stud closures, then shrugged out of the shirt and tossed it aside.

Her hand trembled as she reached out to run her fingers over his padded pectoral muscles and the taut ridges of his abdomen and stomach. The light sprinkling of hair covering his hard flesh tickled her palm and reminded her of the marvelous contrasts between a man and a woman.

When he shuddered from her light touch, she smiled. "Your body is perfect, Josh."

He brought his hands up to brush the stretchy fabric from her shoulders, then kissed the newly exposed skin. "Having you explore my chest feels wonderful, honey. But I want to touch you, too." As he pushed the evening gown down her arms, then over her hips into a shimmery black pool at her feet, Kiley's pulse raced at the look of appreciation in his smoldering blue eyes. When he discovered that she wasn't wearing a bra, his sharp intake of breath caused an interesting little flutter deep in the pit of her stomach. "You're beautiful, Kiley."

Cupping her breasts with his hands, he alternated kissing and teasing her beaded nipples, sending waves of heat sweeping over her. But when he took one of the tight buds into his mouth to explore her with his tongue, the sensations coursing through her were so intense, she felt as if she might faint.

"J-Josh… Oh, my."

"Does that feel good, Kiley?"

Unable to form a coherent thought, all she could do was nod.

"Do you want me to take off the rest of our clothes?" he asked, continuing to taunt the overly sensitive tip.

"Y-yes."

Dressed in nothing but her panties and high heels, she stepped out of the dress at her feet and braced her hands on his shoulders for him to remove her black velvet shoes. When he straightened, she watched him quickly kick off his own shoes, then unzip his tuxedo trousers to shove them and his boxer briefs down his legs. He tossed them and his socks onto the rapidly growing pile of their clothing. When he turned to face her, Kiley's breath lodged in her throat.

She'd been right. Josh's body was—in a word—perfect. His shoulders were impossibly wide, his muscles well-defined and his torso lean. But as her gaze traveled lower, her eyes widened. Josh wasn't just perfect, he was magnificent.

Fully aroused and looking at her as if she were the most desirable creature on earth, he stepped forward to hook his thumbs in the waistband of her lace panties. "I want to feel all of you against me," he said, his intimate tone sending another flash of heat flowing through her.

Once the scrap of silk and lace had been added to the pile of clothes, he took her back into his arms, and the feel of skin against skin caused her knees to give way. He caught her to him and Kiley thought she might go into complete meltdown. His firm, hair-roughened flesh pressed to her smooth feminine skin, the hard length of his erection nestled against her soft belly, set off tiny little sparks skipping over every nerve in her body.

"Honey, I think it would probably be a good idea if we get into bed while we both still have the strength to get there," he said, his warm breath feathering the hair at her temple.

He led her over to the bed and while she pulled back the navy satin duvet and got into bed, he reached into the drawer of the bedside table. Tucking a small foil packet under his pillow, he stretched out beside her and pulled her to him.

"I'm going to try to go slow, honey," he said, giving her a kiss so tender it brought tears to her eyes. "But I've wanted you again for so damned long, I'm not sure that's going to be possible."

"A couple of weeks isn't…all that long," she said, trying to catch her breath.

"I'm not referring to seeing you at the meeting of the funding committee," he said, skimming his hand down her side to her hip. Caressing her thigh, his movements were slow and steady. "I'm talking about how long it's been since we made love the first time. I haven't been able to forget that night three years ago. If I had known your name, I would have tried to find you. But I didn't think asking your sister was the right thing to do, especially since I started distancing myself from her after that night."

His impassioned words created a longing inside of her stronger than anything she had ever experienced before, and she knew that whether she had realized it or not, she had wanted him since that night, as well. But before she could tell him, he parted her to gently touch the tiny nub nestled within and she suddenly felt as if she would go up in flames. His light teasing strokes and the feel of him testing her readiness for him caused a coil of need to tighten deep in the most feminine part of her, and she couldn't stop herself from moving restlessly against him.

Wanting to touch him as he touched her, Kiley slowly slid her hand over his chest, then down his rippled abdomen and beyond. When she found him, her heart skipped several beats at the sheer strength of his need. His body went completely still and a groan rumbled up from deep in his chest as she measured his length and girth with her palm, then explored the softness below.

"Kiley…nothing would make me happier…than to have you touch me like this…for the rest of the night," he said haltingly. When he caught her hands in his, he sounded as if he couldn't take in enough air. "But I want you so damned much…I'm not going to last… if you keep that up."

The look in his eyes sent her temperature soaring, and her need for him grew with each passing second. If they didn't make love soon, she knew for certain she would be reduced to a cinder.

"P-please make love to me, Josh."

He reached under his pillow, quickly arranged their protection, then kissed her with a passion that caused her head to swim. Before she could fully recover, he held her gaze with his as he nudged her knees apart and rose over her.

"Show me where you want me, Kiley," he said, taking her hand in his to place it on his hardened body.

Her heart pounded as she guided him to her and she felt his blunt tip slowly begin to enter her. His gaze never wavered from hers as he eased himself forward and she knew she'd never felt more complete than she did at that moment.

"It feels so good to be inside of you," Josh whispered as he gathered her to him.

Before she could respond, he set a slow pace and Kiley felt as if she were being swept away by the exquisite sensations filling her entire being. Wrapping her arms around his wide shoulders, she held him to her as the coil of need deep within her tightened to the empty ache of unfulfilled desire. But all too soon, she found herself climbing toward the pinnacle, and apparently sensing that she was poised on the edge of finding the satisfaction they both sought, Josh quickened the pace of his lovemaking.

Heat and light flashed behind her tightly closed eyes as she was suddenly set free from the tension holding her captive. Waves of pleasure flowed over her and Kiley had to cling to Josh to keep from being consumed by the exquisite intensity of it all. He thrust into her one final time, then, groaning her name, he joined her in the all-encompassing pleasure of mutual release. As they slowly drifted back to reality it felt as if their souls had been united to become one, and she knew beyond a shadow of doubt that if she hadn't already done so, she was close to losing her heart to the man holding her so securely in his arms.

"You're amazing, honey," he said, kissing her until they both gasped for air.

"That was…breathtaking," she murmured, still trying to come to terms with her newfound realization.

Levering himself to her side, he pulled her close. "Are you all right?"

Deciding there would be plenty of time to analyze her feelings for him later, she kissed his chin. "'All right' doesn't begin to describe how incredible I feel right now, Josh."

She felt his body stir against her leg a moment before a wicked grin appeared on his handsome face. "That's good, because I'm going to spend the rest of the night reminding you of just how incredible we are together."

And to her utter delight, he did just that.

The following Monday afternoon, Kiley gathered some festive paper and a memory stick. "Carrie, will you and Lea be able to watch the children until I get back? I need to walk down to the administrative office to get the programs printed for the Christmas show tomorrow."

"Sure thing." Carrie nodded toward the children sleeping on colorful mats on the floor. "They should nap for another thirty minutes or so. Lea and I can just start story hour a little early if you aren't back when they wake up," she added, referring to the volunteer Kiley hoped to add as a paid staff member after the first of the year.

Nodding, Kiley headed for the door. "I shouldn't be too long."

As she walked down the hall, she couldn't stop thinking about her night with Josh. Never in all of her twenty-eight years had she experienced that level of passion or felt more cherished than she had in his arms. But as wonderful as her night with him had been, once he had taken her back to her place the following morning, reality had intruded as she remembered the unresolved issues between them.

She sighed. He had made it easy to forget that the funding committee would be meeting at the end of the week and she still had no indication if he would recommend additional funds for the day care or side with Beau Hacket and Paul Windsor in hopes of seeing the center close. And then there was the matter of finding the right words to tell him that he was Emmie's father.

If she told him now, how would he react? As fond as he seemed to be of Emmie, Kiley was almost positive he would accept and love her. But her main concern was that he might think she was trying to use her daughter to influence his recommendation to the funding committee. For that matter, it could cross his mind that she had made love with him for that same purpose.

She really didn't think he would consider her making love with him a ploy to keep her job. As if by unspoken agreement, neither of them mentioned the day care center's future when they were away from the TCC clubhouse. But she wasn't so sure he would take the news about Emmie being his child as well. That's why she had made the decision not to tell him until after the funding committee met. If she withheld the information, then there would be no question about her motives. And besides, it wasn't like a couple of days would make a difference. Josh was Emmie's biological father and there wasn't anything that would ever change that fact.

Lost in thought, she paid little attention to the group of teenage boys gathered in one of the alcoves she passed as she walked down the main hallway. At least, she didn't until she heard one of them mention her name.

"I'm telling you it's just a matter of time before that damned Roberts woman and her day care center full of rug rats are history," she heard one of the boys say.

Stopping just out of sight of the sitting area, she shamelessly listened to what the group had to say.

"What makes you think the day care center is going to close, Hack?" another boy asked. "From what I hear it's doing pretty good."

"Well, when it got torn up, my old man said whoever did it had done the club a big favor," Hack said, sounding smug. "He said he had enough influence on the funding committee to see that what the insurance didn't cover would be taken out of the center's budget and that it would run out of money by spring. He even told me he'd thank the vandal if he knew who he was." The boy laughed. "I told him he could just buy me a new truck and we'd call it even."

"You're full of it, Hack," one of the boys scoffed. "There's no way you're the vandal the police are looking for. And your dad wouldn't let you get away with doing something like that here at the TCC."

"Yeah, man, why would you say something like that?" another one asked.

"I know how to work the old fart. He thought I was joking with him." Laughing, the teenager added, "I wanted him in a good mood when I asked for my new ride."

"In other words, he got what he wanted, now you figure he owes you," the scoffer said slowly.

Kiley had heard enough. If what he boasted about was true, Beau Hacket's son had been responsible for the damage done to the day care center. But whether it turned out he was the vandal or not, his claim needed to be investigated.

The Christmas programs forgotten, Kiley walked straight to one of the house phones to have the switchboard operator page Josh. He had stopped by the day care center earlier on his way to lunch with Gil Addison and she hoped they were still in the restaurant or possibly in the bar.

"Josh Gordon here," he said, coming on the line a couple of minutes later.

"I know who vandalized the day care center," Kiley said, careful to keep her voice quiet.

"Kiley?"

"Yes. I just overheard someone bragging about it," she said, deciding not to say the culprit's name aloud for fear of alerting the boys that she had overheard their conversation.

"Where are you?" he asked.

"On the house phone in the main hallway," she answered, keeping an eye on the sitting area. The boys were still there. "Hurry, Josh. He's in a group of teenagers in the alcove across from the Grand Ballroom."

"Gil and I will be right there."

In no time, Josh and Gil came jogging down the hall toward her. "It's Beau Hacket's son," she whispered when they stopped beside her.

"Are you sure?" Josh asked.

She nodded. "The other boys called him Hack and he mentioned his father being on the funding committee."

"It really doesn't surprise me," Gil said, shaking his head. "Hack is a real smart-ass and there isn't a lot I would put past him."

Josh nodded. "And Beau has a blind spot when it comes to that kid. He never makes him face the consequences of his actions."

"Beau isn't going to have a choice this time," Gil said, pointing toward the two plainclothes detectives who had just entered the clubhouse.

"We phoned the police right after you called," Josh explained.

When the detectives joined them, Kiley relayed what she had heard. "They didn't realize I was eavesdropping," she finished.

"Do you know the boys' parents?" the older policeman asked. "They'll need to be called."

"From what he said, I think the Hacket boy acted alone," Kiley said, hoping the other boys weren't deemed guilty by association. They had sounded as appalled at the Hacket boy's claims as she had been.

"We need all of their parents present before we question them," the younger detective advised.

"Since the club has a policy of not allowing anyone underage on the premises without being accompanied by a parent, I'm pretty sure their dads are all here," Gil said, glancing into the alcove. He walked over to the house phone. "I'll have them paged."

While Gil called the switchboard, the police officers walked into the alcove and advised the boys that as soon as their parents arrived, they had some questions they wanted to ask them.

Putting his arm around her shoulders, Josh held Kiley to his side as they walked the short distance to the sitting area. "Are you doing okay, honey?"

"I'm fine," she said, nodding. "I'm just glad we found out who was behind the vandalism and why, even if it was a little disconcerting to hear him admit everything."

"I can't believe he did all that just to make points with his dad in hopes of getting the truck he wanted," Josh said, shaking his head. He grunted. "That kid needs a reality check."

"How do you think Beau will react when he finds out his son was behind all of the destruction?" she asked, checking her watch.

"Knowing Beau, he won't take the news well." Josh shrugged. "But it looks like we aren't going to have to wait to find out."

Looking up, Kiley watched Beau Hacket coming down the hall toward them like a charging bull. "What the hell's going on?" he demanded. If the scowl on his face was any indication, Josh was right about him not taking the news well.

"We know who was behind vandalizing the day care center," Josh answered.

"Who was it?" Beau asked, glancing into the sitting area. The blood drained from his face when he spotted his son among the four boys seated in the alcove. "This had better be some kind of joke."

As the detectives questioned the boys and sorted through the facts, they dismissed all of them but Hack. The teenager didn't look nearly as confident now as he had when the interrogation started.

"Who are you going to believe, Dad? Me or them?" Hack demanded, looking up at his father defiantly.

"Don't lie to me, son," Beau said firmly. "You know I'd never condone you breaking the law."

"I'm telling you, I didn't do it," the boy lied.

"We collected a partial fingerprint when we first investigated the vandalism," the younger policeman advised. "It's enough that once we take you down to the station and fingerprint you, we should be able to establish either your innocence or your guilt."

"I'm going to jail?" Hack asked, looking alarmed for the first time since the detectives arrived. "You're gonna get me out of this, aren't you, Dad? I did it for you," the boy said, unaware that he had just confessed.

"I don't know if I can, son." Beau looked from one detective to the other. "Is there any way to make this right without my boy having a criminal record?"

"It's up to the Texas Cattleman's Club if they want to press charges," the older detective advised. "But we're going to read him his rights and take him down to the station for further questioning. I would suggest you get in touch with your lawyer, Mr. Hacket. Your kid is facing charges of vandalism, criminal mischief and anything else we can think to charge him with." He gave Beau a pointed look. "Although this is the most serious, I don't have to tell you, this isn't the first time he's been in trouble."

Beau looked miserable when he turned to Josh and Gil. "What do you guys think? If I make full restitution for the damages do you think we can let this thing go?" he asked hopefully. "I give you my word I'll do whatever it takes to make this right."

"That's not up to us," Gil said, shaking his head. "This will have to be voted on by the executive board."

"While you all sort this out, we'll take Junior here down to the station." The younger police officer stepped behind Hack to put handcuffs around the teenager's wrists. "You have the right to remain silent...." The detectives led Hack toward the main exit as they continued to read him his rights.

"Can you call an emergency meeting of the board, Gil?" Beau asked, reaching for the cell phone clipped to his belt. Making a quick call to his lawyer, Beau turned back to Josh and Gil. "I can't tell you how much it would mean to me for Hack not to end up with a police record over this."

"Before this goes any further, I have a question for you, Beau," Josh said, folding his arms across his wide chest. "What are you going to do about your son? His complete lack of respect for people and property, as well as his self-discipline, are all but nonexistent. There's going to come a day when you can't pay his way out of the trouble he gets into."

Gil nodded. "I agree with Josh, Beau. I'll call an

emergency meeting for this evening, but if I recommend that the board let you do what you're proposing, we need an assurance from you that something like this won't happen again to us or anyone else in the community."

Surprisingly, instead of getting angry at Josh and Gil for pointing out that something needed to be done with his son, Beau nodded. "I give you my word that he won't be getting into any more trouble. I've threatened to send him to a military school in the past."

"You go on down to the police station with your son and we'll let you know what the board decides," Gil advised.

"There's one more thing that I want done," Josh said as Beau turned to leave.

"What's that?" the man asked, sounding as if he would agree to just about anything.

"When he vandalized the day care center, your son spray-painted a very derogatory word on the wall in reference to Ms. Roberts," Josh stated flatly. "I think an apology is in order. And it had better be sincere."

Beau nodded. "I can't tell you how sorry I am that this happened, Ms. Roberts. Believe me when I say I never intended for my objections to the day care center to cause my son to do something like this. I give you my word, I'll find a way to make this right."

"Apology accepted," Kiley said, suddenly uncomfortable at being the center of attention.

Beau nodded, then turned to Gil and Josh. "I'll be down at the police station. Could you let me know as soon as the board makes a decision?"

Gil nodded. "I'll call you one way or the other."

As they watched Beau hurry toward the exit, Josh

turned to Gil. "While you phone the executive board members, I'm going to walk Kiley back to the day care center," Josh said, putting his arm around her.

"Will you be there tonight for the meeting?" Gil asked as they walked out into the hallway.

Josh wasn't a member of the executive board, but unless it was a closed session, any member in good standing could attend. And since he had witnessed the police's questioning, Kiley wasn't sure he wouldn't be asked to give an account of what had taken place.

"I figure I'll throw my support behind Beau sending Hack off to military school," Josh said, nodding. "I think he could benefit from the discipline and structure of a military academy. It would probably be the best thing that ever happened to that kid."

"At this point, it sure won't hurt," Gil agreed. "And since his dad is one of our own, I'm pretty sure we can get the justice we want without leaving Hack with a criminal record." He smiled at Kiley. "I'll see you a little later this afternoon when I come to get Cade."

"Do you think the board will go along with what you and Gil have in mind?" Kiley asked when Gil left to go back to his office.

Josh nodded as they walked down the hall. "Every member of the TCC is sworn to live by its code— 'Leadership, Justice and Peace.' And we've got a long history of policing our own, as well as righting a lot of injustices for those outside of the club. This is something we can take care of ourselves."

"Hack will be taught a lesson without a criminal record and the club won't suffer further scandal," she guessed.

"That's it. He's seventeen and would have probably

been charged as an adult. This way he'll get the chance to clean up his act without the stigma of having been in trouble with the law." When they stopped at the day care center's door, he took her into his arms. "Thank you for catching him for us."

"I really didn't do anything but eavesdrop." She smiled. "But now that the mystery is solved, I'm glad I won't have to worry about coming in to work one morning and finding the place destroyed again."

He gave her a long, deep kiss. "Now that I have that meeting, I won't be able to see you until sometime tomorrow."

"Are you planning on attending the children's Christmas program tomorrow afternoon?" she asked, feeling the familiar flutter of desire begin deep in the pit of her belly.

"Of course." His deep chuckle caused the fluttering inside of her to go berserk. "I wouldn't think of missing the pony princess's singing debut."

Kiley's chest swelled with emotion. "She's going to be thrilled to see you there."

"I think Gil said the program is in the main ballroom?" he asked.

"Yes."

He nodded and gave her a quick kiss. "I'll call you this evening and let you know the outcome of the board's vote."

As she watched Josh walk away, Kiley caught her lower lip between her teeth to keep it from trembling. Any doubts she had about him accepting Emmie as his daughter had just been erased. Very few men would make sure they attended a toddler's Christmas program if they didn't care a great deal for the child. And once he learned he was Emmie's father, Kiley believed he would be the loving daddy that her daughter had always deserved.

But where did she fit into the equation?

Kiley knew that he liked kissing her and there was no doubt he desired her. But could he ever love her?

Her heart stalled and it suddenly became difficult to draw her next breath. She had known the night they made love that she was in danger of doing it, but had she actually fallen for him?

Knowing in her heart that was exactly what had happened, she slowly opened the door to the day care center. She wasn't comfortable with it and it certainly added another wrinkle to an already complicated situation. But there was no denying it, either.

Whether she liked it or not, she had fallen head over heels in love with Josh Gordon.

Nine

The next afternoon, Josh stopped his SUV at the TCC clubhouse entrance, got out and tossed the keys to one of the valets. He had just enough time to find himself a seat in the Grand Ballroom before the day care center's Christmas program started.

If anyone had told him a few weeks ago that he would be rushing to attend something put on by a bunch of little kids, he would have questioned their sanity. But now? He'd walk through hell if he had to in order to keep from disappointing one cute little girl and her beautiful mother.

He frowned as a woman standing by the door to the ballroom handed him a program with a brightly colored holiday design. When had Kiley and Emmie become so important to him? And how had it happened so quickly?

His mouth went as dry as a wad of cotton as he entered the ballroom and found himself a seat. Surely he hadn't fallen in love with Kiley. He knew he liked her a lot and the chemistry between them was nothing short of amazing. But love?

Giving himself a mental shake, he almost laughed out loud at his own foolishness. He had to be losing it. There wasn't any question that he was in lust with the woman. But that didn't mean he was in love with her.

And he could even understand his feelings for Emmie. She was a cute, friendly little girl and it would take a heartless bastard not to find her completely adorable.

He sat down next to an older couple close to the front of the portable stage that had been set up next to the Christmas tree. Seeing the decorated tree, he couldn't help but think about dancing with Kiley the night of the ball. That one dance had been all it took for them to decide to leave the gala and go back to his place for the most incredible night he'd spent in the past three years.

"We're here to see our grandson," the woman said, smiling. "And you?"

Before he could tell the beaming grandmother he was a friend of the day care center's director and her little girl, Christmas music filled the room and the kids began to take their places on the stage. When he spotted Emmie in her red velvet dress, pigtails bobbing as she skipped along, he couldn't stop grinning. She had to be the cutest kid ever.

As the program began, there were several times Josh found himself laughing out loud. Kiley and her helpers had to lead wandering kids back to their places, hand giant plastic candy canes back to the little ones who dropped theirs and take a giant bell away from one of the preschool boys when he used it to bop one of the little girls on the head. Josh enjoyed the program immensely and he was certain the rest of the crowd had, too.

When the kids sang the last song, Kiley thanked everyone for attending, told the parents that the day care was dismissed for the rest of the afternoon and then motioned for Josh to come up to the stage. "Would you mind watching Emmie for a moment while I get everything cleared up here?" she asked.

"No problem," he said, picking up the toddler. "We'll be over by the tree."

As he carried her over to look at the decorative ornaments on the tree, he marveled at the fact that he was actually watching after a kid and didn't mind it at all. "Did you see this ornament, Emmie?" he asked, pointing to Santa's sleigh with eight tiny reindeer hanging from one of the branches.

"Ponies," Emmie said, her little face beaming as she pointed at it.

Tickling her tummy, he laughed. "You've got a one-track mind, princess."

"Your daughter is very cute," the woman who had sat next to him throughout the program said as she and her husband walked over with their grandson in tow. "She looks just like you." Josh smiled and started to correct her, but the woman didn't give him the chance. "Do you have a cell phone?" she asked.

"Yes, do you need to use it?" He unclipped his phone from his belt and handed it to her.

"I'll use the camera on your phone to take your

picture with her here by the tree, if you'll return the favor and take one of us with our grandson," she said, pulling a digital camera from her purse.

"Sure," Josh agreed. He wouldn't mind having a picture of himself and Emmie, and if the woman wanted to think they looked alike, what would it hurt?

After the pictures had been taken and the couple moved on, he checked the gallery on his phone to see how the photo had turned out. He smiled at the image. Perched in the crook of his arm, Emmie had her hand resting on his cheek and the sweetest grin he had ever seen on her cute little face.

But his smile suddenly faded as he looked at his image and then Emmie's. He normally didn't pay any attention to who resembled who. He had a mirror image of himself in his twin brother, Sam, and didn't figure he looked like anyone else. Staring at the picture suddenly had him changing his mind.

He had never before seen himself and Emmie together—not in a mirror or a picture. And since he hadn't been looking for any similarities between the two of them, he hadn't given it so much as a fleeting thought. But there was no denying that Emmie looked a lot like him. He could see glimpses of Kiley in Emmie's big brown eyes and the delicate shape of her face, but the child had his nose and smile. And their hair color was almost exactly the same shade.

"Did you enjoy the program?" Kiley asked, walking up to them.

Looking up, he clipped the phone back on his belt as he nodded. "Are you finished for the day?"

"Yes. The children have all been turned over to their parents and the props have been stored in my office," she said as she took Emmie from him to set her on her feet. Helping the little girl into her coat, she zipped it up. "Would you like to come over and help us bake and decorate sugar cookies for the rest of the afternoon?"

Suddenly needing to put space between them, Josh shook his head. "I'll have to take a rain check on that. I need to get back to one of the job sites," he lied. What he needed was time to think.

"We'll save some for you," she said, oblivious to the turmoil beginning to roil through him.

He nodded. "I'll see you tomorrow."

"At the meeting of the funding committee?" she asked.

"Yeah." He kissed Kiley's cheek and the top of Emmie's head, then started toward the exit to the ball-room.

As he walked out of the clubhouse and got into his SUV, he sat there for several long minutes staring blindly at the steering wheel. He knew Kiley had expected him to at least drop by that evening after he finished with his duties at Gordon Construction. But he needed time to think, time to do some calculating and then decide what he was going to do.

Beyond learning how to protect himself and his partner when they made love, he hadn't paid much attention in sex education class. Hell, he couldn't think of a teenage boy who did. They all had more hormones than good sense and were too busy hoping to get lucky with one of the cheerleaders to give things like the gestation of a woman's pregnancy a lot of thought. But it didn't take a Rhodes scholar to figure out that there was more than just a possibility, there was a very real probability, that the cute little girl he called the pony princess was his daughter.

Standing in the hall outside of the meeting room, Kiley dried her sweaty palms on her khaki slacks as she tried to think of what she could say this time to convince the members to approve the increase in the day care center's budget that she hadn't gone over the last time they'd met. Of course, when Josh gave her the money to cover one month of the extra funds she'd asked for, he had promised that if he saw a need for the TCC day care center, he would personally recommend that the committee approve her request. But he hadn't mentioned making a decision and she hadn't asked.

"Ms. Roberts, the committee is ready to see you now." When she looked up, one of the members was holding the door for her to enter the meeting room.

As she walked up to the conference table, Josh was busy entering notes into his electronic tablet and barely raised his head to acknowledge her presence. A sinking feeling began to settle in the pit of her stomach.

"Ms. Roberts, have your needs for the day care center changed since our last meeting with you?" he asked, finally looking at her.

Confused by his all-business tone and cool demeanor, she shook her head. "No, I still need the extra money to supplement what the committee has already appropriated for the center."

Why was he acting so indifferent to the situation? He had stopped by the center enough times to know what the funds would be used for and that if she didn't get them the TCC day care center would have to close by spring.

He gave her a short nod. "I'm going to excuse my-self from the discussion and vote because of our re-lationship, but I'll come down to the day care center after the meeting is over to let you know the outcome."

Effectively dismissed, there was nothing left for her to do but go back to the center and wait for Josh to explain himself. But as she walked back to the center she felt her cheeks heat as her anger rose.

She could understand that he had no choice but to excuse himself from the issue because of a conflict of interest. But surely he could have given his report on what he had observed of the day-to-day running of the center. And why was he acting so aloof? Was it his way of telling her that she had little or no chance for additional funding? If that was the case, the day care center would be closing down shortly after the first of the year.

"Merry Christmas, Kiley," she muttered sarcasti-cally.

As soon as the holidays were over, she would have to start looking for another job. She had no doubt she could find something at another day care center, but she would have to accept whatever position they had open and she could only hope that it paid well enough for her to make ends meet for herself and Emmie.

By the time Josh opened the door and entered the day care center an hour later, Kiley wasn't certain she wanted to hear the official outcome of the vote. At least not until after the holidays were over.

"Let's go into your office," he suggested.

Nodding, she led the way to the former storage room that served as her office. When he closed the door behind them, she shook her head. "You don't have to tell me the outcome of the funding committee's vote," she said, sitting in the hard wooden desk chair. "I knew when I was summarily dismissed what the outcome would be." She took a deep breath in an effort to calm herself. "What I'd like to know is what these past few weeks have been about, since you clearly never intended to recommend additional funding for the day care center."

"The issue was tabled until a later date. But before we get into that, I have a couple of questions for you." His eyes narrowed. "Are you aware that I'm Emmie's father?"

Thrown off guard by his unexpected question, she slowly nodded. "Y-yes."

"Is that why your ex-husband refused to have anything to do with her? Did he know or suspect that she wasn't his child?" he demanded.

"No. As far as Mark is concerned, he still thinks he fathered her." Anticipating his next question, she met his angry gaze head-on. "And before you ask, I didn't realize it was even a possibility until you came by my house that first night with the pizza. That's when I noticed that Emmie looks a lot like you."

He rose to his feet to pace the small area in front of her desk. "Why didn't you tell me as soon as you suspected it was a possibility?"

"I wanted to confirm my suspicions before I talked to you about it," she defended herself.

His eyes narrowed. "And you've done that?"

She stood up to face him. "Yes."

"When?"

"The day I went to lunch with Piper, I saw my ex-husband in the Royal Diner and asked him about his blood type." She shook her head. "I had done enough research on the internet to know immediately that there was no way Mark could be her biological father."

Josh stopped pacing to glare at her. "That was a week ago, Kiley. What were you waiting on? Didn't you think I had the right to know I have a daughter?"

"Oh, no, you don't, buster," she fumed, walking up to stand toe to toe with him. "You're not going to make me feel guilty about not telling you right away that Emmie is your child. Not when I was doing everything I knew how to do to keep from making you think I was trying to use her to influence your recommendation to the funding committee." She poked him in the chest with her finger. "But I shouldn't have bothered because you never intended to give the day care center a fair chance anyway, did you?" She turned away, then whirled back to add, "And just for the record, I intended to tell you as soon as the funding committee made a final decision and settled the day care center's fate once and for all. That way I couldn't be accused of something I wasn't guilty of."

"Let's leave the day care center out of this for the moment," he hissed. "I want to finish talking about my daughter."

"Our daughter," Kiley corrected. "And there's really nothing to discuss. I won't try to stop you from being part of Emmie's life, if that's what you want. But I have two conditions before I'll agree to anything."

His expression was dark and guarded. "What kind of conditions?"

"I don't want your money to help support her. I'm perfectly capable of providing for my child."

"Our child," he reminded. "And let me make one

thing perfectly clear right now. It will be a cold day in hell before you tell me what I will or won't do to see that she's taken care of."

Kiley counted to ten as she tried to keep tears from welling in her eyes. How could she love him so much when she was so darned angry with him? So disillusioned?

"We can cover that another time," she finally managed to get out around the lump clogging her throat. "The most important stipulation I have is that you love her. Emmie deserves that and if you can't be the daddy she needs, I'd rather you not try to have a relationship with her at all."

A muscle worked furiously along his jaw. "I can't believe you think I would do otherwise." Staring hard at her for what seemed like an eternity, he finally turned and opened the door to her office. "We'll talk about this later when we're both thinking more clearly."

Through the office window looking out into the day care center, Kiley watched Josh march across the room and leave before she walked back around her desk on shaky legs. Sinking into her chair, she buried her face in her hands. Even before her sister had admitted that Josh wasn't the snake she'd led their family to believe, Kiley's instincts had told her that he wasn't a bad guy. Had she been wrong about him? Was she destined to be like her sister and see traits in a man that simply weren't there? Why hadn't he been able to see that she had handled the situation the best way she knew how?

A sudden thought had her sitting up straight in the chair. Could Josh have gotten the issue of the day care center tabled as a way of retaliation? Was he getting even with her for not telling him when she first suspected that he was Emmie's father?

She wasn't sure. But a day care center full of children wasn't the place to have an emotional meltdown. There would be plenty of time for that when she got home and let go of the tight grip she held on her emotions.

Feeling as if her heart had been shattered into a million pieces, Kiley did her best to pull herself together. Fate may have set her and Josh on a path three years ago with the conception of Emmie that would entwine their lives forever, but that didn't mean she was going to let it break her. She was a survivor. She had made it through the inevitable end of her disastrous marriage and the emotional pain of seeing her child rejected by the man she'd thought until recently was Emmie's father. She could certainly weather having her heart broken by Josh Gordon's deceit and betrayal.

She straightened her shoulders, stood up and with a smile firmly in place, walked out into the day care. She might be suffering from a broken heart that she was certain could never be mended, as well as facing the probability of losing her dream job in a few months, but until then, she had parents and children who were counting on her. And she wasn't going to let them down.

Sitting in his darkened family room, Josh took a swig from the half-empty beer bottle in his hand as he stared at the Christmas tree he and his daughter had put up during the ice storm. His daughter. He tightly closed his eyes as a wave of emotion surged through him. Dear God, he had a child.

The mere thought had him running his hand over his face in an attempt to wipe away the tangled feelings that had threatened to swamp him since discovering Emmie was his daughter. He had been crazy about the kid before. But now that he knew she belonged to him—that she was his own flesh and blood—it caused a tightness in his chest that was almost debilitating. He had never felt such love in his entire life and it had been almost instantaneous.

And then there were his feelings for her mother. What he had thought to be nothing more than a strong case of lust had turned out to be far more than he could have ever imagined.

His heart slammed into his rib cage with the force of a physical blow and he had to take several deep breaths as he gave in and acknowledged the emotion that he had avoided putting a name to. He'd fallen hopelessly in love with Kiley and he hadn't even seen it coming.

He'd known that he wanted to spend all of his time with her and that he desired her more than he had any woman in his entire life. But not once had it occurred to him that he was falling in love with her.

As the certainty of the emotion settled in, he knew he wanted to be the man to hold her while she slept at night, wanted to wake up with her each morning and spend the rest of his life spoiling her the way her jerk of an ex-husband never had. He wanted to help her raise Emmie and wanted to give her more babies for them to love and enjoy.

Unfortunately, he was almost positive he had destroyed any possibility of her ever allowing him to do that when he'd refused to talk to her about it further.

And he really couldn't say he blamed her. They had things they needed to work out and spending the past few days holed up in his house brooding about it all wasn't accomplishing anything.

"You blew it, Gordon," he muttered miserably as he opened his eyes to stare at the bottle in his hand.

Drinking the last of the beer, he set the empty bottle down on the end table next to the other three he had polished off earlier. He had overreacted to the entire situation when he'd confronted her at the day care center and driven the only woman he had ever loved—would ever love—from his life. Most likely for good.

Josh sighed heavily. Now that he'd had a few days to cool down and started looking at things rationally, he could understand Kiley's wanting to be positive about who had fathered Emmie before she approached him about it. It just made good sense to handle it that way.

He could even appreciate her reasoning for not wanting to tell him until after the funding committee decided on the additional funds for the day care center, too. She hadn't wanted there to be any question about her motives. He respected and admired that kind of integrity.

And although her fears were unfounded, he even got why she was afraid he wouldn't step up to the plate and be the father Emmie needed. She was trying to protect her child—their child—and there was no way in hell he would ever fault her for that. He would be disappointed in her if she didn't.

As he sat there staring at the twinkling lights on the tree, he thought back over the past few weeks. Spending time with her and Emmie had given him a glimpse of what his life with them could be like, and he wanted that more than he wanted his next breath.

He smiled through the mist of emotion gathering in his eyes. He'd enjoyed the nights they spent together eating in front of the television while they watched a movie, even if it had been the same cartoon both times. Then, after the pony princess was tucked into bed for the night, he loved sitting on the couch with Kiley, holding her close, talking to her and kissing her until they both gasped for breath.

He had even loved taking on the responsibility of being their protector. Initially, Kiley hadn't appreciated his insistence that he drive her and Emmie to his place to ride out the ice storm. But just the thought of her having an accident on the icy roads or either one of them being cold and uncomfortable in a house without heat and electricity had been more than he could bear.

Sighing heavily, he uttered a curse word that he only used around the guys or when he did something stupid like smash his thumb with a hammer. He loved them both unconditionally and that was something that would never change. But he was afraid he had come to that realization too late.

Unable to sit still, he stood up, gathered the beer bottles and went outside to the shed to toss them in the recycle bin. Standing in his backyard, he stared up at the star-studded night sky. He wanted it all—Kiley, Emmie and to be the best husband and father he could possibly be. But what could he do to get them back to where they had been, to make things right between him and Kiley?

He wasn't sure there was anything he could do to repair the damage he had caused to their relationship.

But the one thing he did know for certain was that he had to try. If he didn't, he knew as surely as the sun rose in the east each morning, he would regret it every second of every day for the rest of his life.

Ten

Two days before Christmas, Kiley sat in her living room watching Emmie play with the pony castle her grandparents had given her the night Kiley and Josh went to the Christmas Ball. She had spent a miserable few days wondering how she could have handled the situation with Josh any differently. After going over everything time and again, she had come to the conclusion that she couldn't.

Telling him about her suspicions before she had concrete evidence would have definitely made it appear as if she had some sort of agenda to use Emmie to keep the day care center open, as well as made her look utterly foolish if it had turned out he wasn't. Or he might have even thought she was somehow trying to extort money from him to support a child who wasn't his.

Sighing, she rose from the chair and walked into the kitchen to put her coffee cup in the dishwasher. To a point, she could understand Josh's angry reaction. Learning that he had a two-year-old child had to have been a huge shock. But that was no reason not to give her explanation serious consideration.

And then there was his promise to give the day care center a fair evaluation. Why hadn't he reported his observations and then excused himself from the vote for the additional funds for the facility? He knew that was the only chance the day care center had to survive. The only reasons she could think of to explain his actions were either he hadn't been impressed with the services she was providing to the children of the TCC members or he was retaliating against her for not telling him about Emmie. And that hurt almost as much as his unwillingness to listen to her.

Lost in thought, she jumped when the phone rang. It was probably her parents, asking her what time she thought she and Emmie would be arriving Christmas day to exchange gifts. But when she checked, the Texas Cattleman's Club number was displayed on the caller ID.

"Kiley, I'm sorry to bother you, but we need you here at the clubhouse," Gil Addison said when she answered.

"Is something wrong?" she asked. Now that Beau Hacket's son had been dealt with over the vandalism and was scheduled to attend a military school in central Texas immediately after the first of the year, she hoped nothing else had happened to the day care center.

"No," he assured her. "We just need to talk to you about your future employment here at the club."

Great, on top of everything else, they were going to fire her two days before Christmas. "I'll be there—" she glanced at the clock "—in about an hour."

"That will be great," he said, sounding cheerful. "We'll see you then."

When he hung up, she stared at the phone. She had thought Gil was quite happy with the job she was doing. Now it appeared he was happy to be rid of her.

Getting herself and Emmie ready to face the inevitable, she wondered why the TCC had decided to terminate her contract early, instead of waiting until it closed the day care center in the spring. "Your daddy probably had something to do with that," she said without thinking.

"Daddy?" Emmie asked, clearly confused. She looked around the room as if searching for something.

"No, sweetie," Kiley said, mentally chiding herself as they left the house and she strapped Emmie into her car seat. Two-year-olds tended to parrot everything they heard and since he hadn't come around them in the past few days, she had no idea if Josh intended to be a real father to Emmie or not. "Mommy made a mistake."

Twenty minutes later when she drove into the club-house parking lot, she recognized several cars and couldn't help but wonder why Piper and Ryan were at the club. She thought they were busy making final wedding arrangements. In fact, she thought everyone would be busy with last-minute shopping or traveling to spend the holidays with family.

"We might as well get this over with, Emmie," she said, lifting her daughter from the car seat to walk up to the front door.

The door opened before she could reach for the handle. "I'm glad you were able to make it on short notice," Piper said, grinning.

Kiley frowned. "What are you doing here?"

"They've called an emergency meeting of the funding committee," Piper said, hurrying her down the hall to the ballroom. "I'm here to give you moral support."

Before they entered the room, Kiley set Emmie on her feet to remove their coats. "Ryan isn't on the committee," she commented as she straightened. "What's really going on, Piper?"

"Ryan's here to support you, too." Her friend smiled mysteriously. "So are the majority of the parents who have kids in the day care center."

"Piper, I appreciate their support, but I doubt it will make a difference," she said tiredly. She hadn't slept well since arguing with Josh and didn't anticipate her insomnia getting better any time soon.

"Come on." Piper urged her toward the closed ballroom doors. "This won't take long. I promise."

Taking Emmie by the hand, Kiley opened the door to the big room, walked inside and looked around. Tables had been set up on the stage the day care had used and the funding committee members were seated behind them, looking at her expectantly.

Most of the parents and their children from the day care center sat in rows of chairs in front of the stage, and she was grateful for their support even though it probably wouldn't influence the committee's vote.

"Ms. Roberts, would you please approach the committee?" Josh asked, drawing her attention to him.

She had purposely avoided looking at him when she entered the room. But as she turned her attention his way, her breath caught. Instead of a suit and tie like the other male members on the panel were wearing, he was dressed in boots, jeans and a chambray shirt. She didn't think he had ever looked as handsome as he did at that moment. But why was he dressed so casually?

Walking up to the front of the room, she was surprised when Josh grinned and stood up. "It would be a conflict of interest for me to preside over this meeting, as well as vote on the future of the day care center. For that reason, I'm excusing myself," he said, handing the gavel to Beau Hacket. "I do, however, retain my right to report my observations on the center's operation and give my recommendation of action on the issue." He walked to the end of the stage, descended the steps and came to stand beside her.

"What's going on?" she demanded under her breath.

"Just wait," he whispered close to her ear.

"Can we at least sit down?" she asked. Why did they have to humiliate her by firing her in front of everyone?

"No. Just listen," he said, smiling at her. Her heart skipped a beat at the warmth she detected in his brilliant blue eyes.

"Up," Emmie said, patting Josh's leg.

Without a moment's hesitation, he picked up their daughter and held her close. "How's my little princess?" he asked, causing Kiley's chest to swell with emotion. Even if he couldn't care for her, there was no doubt how he felt about their daughter. It was easy to see Josh loved their daughter with all his heart.

"It's been brought to our attention that the funding committee needs to review our calculations for the day care center's budget," Beau stated, drawing everyone's attention back to the panel of men. "We've also been asked by Gil Addison to review Ms. Roberts's contract for the position of day care center operator."

Here it comes, Kiley thought. This was where they were going to terminate her contract. But why did they have to ruin Christmas for her and Emmie? Why couldn't they have waited until after the first of the year?

"I make a motion to start the discussion," Paul Windsor said when Beau gave him a nod.

When one of the other members seconded the motion, Beau looked directly at Josh. "I think you have something to report?"

Josh nodded and, with Emmie perched on his forearm, stepped forward. "After Ms. Roberts addressed the committee at the first of the month requesting additional funds for the day care center, I made periodic visits to see how she was running the operation and to determine if the money was actually needed."

"And what were your findings?" Beau asked, surprising Kiley with his even tone and pleasant expression. Apparently, his way of "making things right" for what his son had done was to at least appear interested and congenial.

"I've observed Ms. Roberts in several different situations at the day care center and I can honestly say I was extremely impressed by her dedication and how well she was able to relate to the kids," he said, making eye contact with every one of the panel members. "She gives each child individual attention and makes them all feel like everything they show or tell her is of the utmost importance. I've also observed her methods of discipline and I was amazed by the kindness and respect she showed." He chuckled. "The little boy in question happily accepted his 'time out' without protest or her having to raise her voice above normal." He turned to look at her and the expression on his handsome face was breathtaking. "And I doubt anyone could have done a better job of putting on an entertaining and enjoyable children's Christmas program."

The crowd of parents broke their silence with applause and several even called out words of encouragement and support.

When the parents quieted down, he continued, "In conclusion, I would like to add that the TCC has a top-notch day care center." His gaze never wavered from hers. "And we have the dedication and expertise of Kiley Roberts to thank for it. I recommend that you vote to keep the day care center open and appropriate the funds needed to keep it running."

"I would like to add that I think the TCC should renegotiate her contract to include a raise and a five-year extension," Gil Addison said, walking up to stand beside Josh.

The group of parents once again erupted in a round of applause and loud cheers.

Tears filled her eyes and Kiley couldn't have found her voice to save her soul. Josh's heartfelt endorsement was more than she could have possibly hoped for and proved that no matter what their differences were, he wasn't going to hold them against the club's day care center.

"Thank you," she mouthed, looking at the only man she would ever love. She just wished their problems could be resolved as easily as the fate of the day care center. Unfortunately, she wasn't sure that was going to be the case.

Beau banged the gavel to bring order back to the meeting. "Are there any other comments?"

"My son, Cade, has learned more at the TCC day care center in the past couple of months than he ever did at the child care facility he used to attend," Gil stated.

"All of the children love Miss Kiley," Winnie Bartlett added. "My daughters are disappointed on the weekends when they can't go to school."

"I move to adopt Josh Gordon's recommendations," the only female on the panel said, grinning.

"I second the motion," one of the men chimed in.

"Then I guess all there is left to do would be to bring it to a vote," Beau said, smiling. "All those in favor of the recommendations set forth by Josh Gordon and Gil Addison, please raise your hands."

When every member of the funding committee, including Beau and his cohort Paul Windsor, raised their hands high in the air, Beau nodded. "It's unanimous. The motion carries," he said, bringing down the gavel to seal the fate of the day care center.

Kiley couldn't believe what had just taken place. She had been summoned to the TCC clubhouse, expecting to be fired. Now she had job security for the next five years, as well as a raise.

Amid the thunderous cheers and standing ovation, Beau Hacket pounded the gavel on the table several times. "Order, please." He looked at Josh. "I think there's something else Josh wants to say."

She frowned. What on earth could he possibly have to add?

Still holding Emmie, Josh took Kiley by the hand and led her up onto the stage. Kiley's heart pounded so hard, she wasn't sure it wouldn't create a hole in her chest. What was he up to now?

"The reason I felt it would be a conflict of interest for me to preside over the meeting today was because, as many of you know, I've been seeing Kiley for the past few weeks," he stated, glancing down at her. His smile and the light she detected in his eyes caused her to feel warm all over. "I didn't feel I could vote without bias on an issue that involves the woman I love."

As the crowd clapped their approval, Kiley looked at Piper, standing with her fiancé, Ryan Grant. Smiling, tears filled her friend's eyes. "It's going to work out, Kiley," she mouthed. "I'm so happy for you."

Feeling as if she were in a bizarre dream, Kiley looked up at Josh. They still had problems. But for the first time in days, she felt there might be a glimmer of hope that things could work out between them, at least where Emmie was concerned.

"There's one more thing before we adjourn," Josh said, quieting the well-wishers. "I'd like to thank you all for coming to the club on such short notice to support Kiley and the day care center."

He grinned and whispered close to her ear, "Now let's get out of here. I have something at the ranch I want to show Emmie and we have some things we need to talk over."

They were silent as they made their way through the crowd to the clubhouse parking lot, and by the time they reached his SUV, Kiley felt as if she had regained some of her equilibrium. Josh had taken her by surprise when he made the recommendations for the day care center and his public announcement that he loved her had caused her head to spin. But now that she was able to think more clearly, her cautious nature took over. Just because he said he loved her didn't mean things would automatically work out for them.

Parking the truck by the corral gate, Josh looked over at the woman in the passenger seat beside him. Kiley was the only woman he had ever loved—would ever love. And he had to make things right between them.

"Thank you for allowing me to bring the two of you out here to the ranch," he said, reaching over to take her hand in his. "I wanted to give Emmie her Christmas present."

Kiley nodded, looking cautious. "I'm sure she'll love whatever you have for her."

He had hurt her emotionally and she was being careful. He could understand that and he didn't blame her one bit. He had been a complete jackass and he wasn't fool enough to think that telling her he loved her in front of a crowd was going to make everything okay. It was going to take some serious groveling on his part to make it up to her. He was prepared to do that and whatever else it took to get her to give him another chance.

"Wanna see ponies," Emmie chimed in from the backseat. Apparently she had recognized the barn when he stopped the truck.

"I think that can be arranged, princess," he said, smiling in the rearview mirror at the most precious little girl in the entire world. She and her mother were his whole world, and if Kiley would give him the chance, he would spend every minute of every day proving it to them.

Getting out of the Navigator, he came around the front to open Kiley's door and help her down from the seat. Then, getting Emmie from her car seat, he set her on her feet. "Are you ready to see the ponies?"

Emmie clapped her hands. "Pet a pony."

"You can do more than pet a pony," Josh said, smiling. "You can ride one."

Her little face lit up with glee as she nodded. "Wanna wide."

"We're not dressed for horseback riding," Kiley said, frowning. "Was that the reason you were dressed so casually for the meeting? You intended to go for a ride afterward?"

He shrugged. "I'm not going riding, but since a suit and tie aren't appropriate attire for a barnyard, I figured jeans were my best bet."

"I don't understand," Kiley said, looking confused.

"Emmie's Christmas present is in the barn," he said, grinning.

Kiley shook her head. "You didn't."

He nodded. "I sure did. My daughter likes ponies, she gets a pony."

"You're going to spoil her, Josh Gordon."

"That's my intention." He wanted to tell Kiley he intended to spoil her, too, but that would have to wait until a little later.

When Bobby Ray led the fat Shetland pony from the barn, already saddled and ready to ride, the look on Emmie's face was one Josh knew he would never forget. "Pony! Pony!" his daughter chanted excitedly.

"This is Rosy," he said, lifting Emmie to set her on the saddle. "She's your pony."

"Me pony?" The child's delight was priceless and he wouldn't have traded seeing it for the entire world.

Strapping a blue toddler-size riding helmet on her head, Josh walked beside the pony as he led her around the corral several times until he noticed Martha waiting at the corral fence. He had made arrangements in advance for his housekeeper to watch Emmie while he tried to straighten out things with Kiley.

Lifting his daughter down, he handed the lead rope back to Bobby Ray. "You can ride again a little later, princess. Do you think you could go with Martha now and have some lunch while I talk to your mommy?"

Grinning, Emmie waved as she and Martha walked toward the house. "Bye-bye."

"She's amazing, Kiley," he said, staring after their little girl. "You've done a wonderful job with her."

"She's my world," Kiley said, smiling for the first time since they left the TCC clubhouse.

"Do you have room in that world of yours for me?" he asked, gently touching her smooth cheek.

"Josh, please…" she said, starting to turn away from him. "I don't want to hear it if you don't mean it."

Reaching out, he pulled her into his arms. She tried to push away from him, but he locked his arms around her. He was determined to settle things between them. It was the only possible chance they had of building a future together.

"Kiley, don't just quit on us." Placing his finger beneath her chin, he tilted her head until their gazes met. "I know I hurt you, but hear me out before you make the decision to walk away from what we have together."

She stared at him for several long seconds before she spoke. "Besides Emmie, just what do you think we have, Josh?"

"Love," he answered. "I love you and you love me. And it's something I have every intention of fighting for. I meant it when I announced it at the meeting. I love you, Kiley."

"You didn't feel that way the other day." She shook her head. "You walked out in the middle of quite possibly the most important conversation we'll ever have—the one about our daughter."

The emotional pain and disappointment he saw in the depths of her pretty brown eyes made him feel as if he'd been punched in the gut. But it was no less than he deserved.

"I know I acted like a complete bastard, and I regret that more than you'll ever know," he said honestly. "I left because I needed time to come to grips with everything. I know it's no excuse for my behavior or the accusations I hurled at you, but it's the truth. I was never more shocked in my entire life than I was when I figured out Emmie is mine. But what angered me the most was that you knew and didn't tell me as soon as you suspected I could be her father."

"I didn't want to be an alarmist in case I was wrong," she said defensively. "Nor did I want you to think I was using Emmie to try to keep the day care open."

He nodded. "I understand that now that I've had time to think straight. And I admire you for handling it the way you did. But at the time, all I could think was that you'd deceived me."

"And I felt you had betrayed me when you put off the day care issue at the funding meeting," she shot back. "You had assured me you were going to give the day care center a fair evaluation. But that afternoon you acted like it was an inconvenience for me to even request the additional funds."

"To tell you the truth, the day care center was the last thing on my mind at that point," he said, meaning it. "I asked that the issue of additional funding be tabled because I figured with my state of mind, it was the only fair thing I could do."

"Why did you call an emergency meeting of the funding committee today to decide the day care's fate?" she asked, frowning. "Couldn't it have waited until after the first of the year?"

"I wanted to make sure that issue was dealt with and out of the way so I could concentrate on fixing the mess I had made with you." He brushed her lips with his. When she didn't protest, he took that as a positive sign and went on. "I love you, Kiley. And I take full responsibility for our argument." He kissed her forehead. "If you'll let me, I want to spend the rest of my life making it up to you for acting the way I did."

As she stared up at him, tears filled her eyes, and knowing he had caused her to cry made him feel as if someone tried to rip out his heart. "Josh, you don't have to say that." She shook her head. "I'm not going to try to stop you from being with Emmie."

"Honey, I know that." Giving her a kiss that had her clinging to him for support and him feeling as if his jeans had become too small in the stride, he smiled.

"What I'm trying to tell you is that I don't just want Emmie. I want you, too. I love you more than life itself. I want to marry you and raise a whole house full of kids just like our beautiful little girl."

"Josh, I don't know—"

"Do you love me, Kiley?"

Tears streamed down her cheeks as she nodded.

"Will you marry me?"

"I—I'm not sure—"

Kissing her again, he felt like he'd run a marathon by the time he raised his head. "Are you sure now?"

"I—I… You're not making it easy to think," she said, looking delightfully confused.

"Just say yes, Kiley," he commanded.

As she continued to look at him, he could tell the moment she gave in to what he knew they both wanted. "Y-yes."

"Thank God!" Releasing her, he reached into the front pocket of his jeans and pulled out the red velvet box he had carried with him since stopping by the jewelry store on the way to the TCC clubhouse earlier that morning. "Kiley, will you marry me?"

Laughing, she covered her mouth with both hands. "You already asked me that and I said yes."

"Say it again." He laughed as he opened the box, removed the one-carat solitaire diamond ring inside and slipped it on her finger. "And keep saying it until we celebrate our seventy-fifth wedding anniversary."

"Yes, I'll marry you, Josh Gordon," she said, throwing her arms around his neck.

"Good." He gave her a quick kiss, then, taking her by the hand, led her toward the house.

"Are we going to tell Emmie?" she asked.

"No. We can tell her later, after we've talked to your folks. I know they're going to have a lot of tough questions about my being Emmie's father and how that all came about." He kissed the top of her head. "But we'll do that together."

"Will you go with me to their place on Christmas Day?" she asked.

He nodded. "We can go to Midland to see your parents and on the way back home, we can stop by and tell my brother that we're going to be a family. But right now, I have something else in mind." He chuckled as he closed the corral gate behind them. "And standing in the middle of a barnyard isn't exactly the place I want to do it."

"You're incorrigible, Josh Gordon," she said, laughing with him.

"No, honey. I'm a man in love with the most desirable woman on the planet," he said, pulling her back into his arms for another kiss.

"I love you, Josh," she said softly.

"And I love you, Kiley." Grinning, he took her hand in his. "Now let's go inside the house and get started planning our life together."

* * * * *

COMING NEXT MONTH FROM

HARLEQUIN

Desire

Available January 7, 2014

#2275 FOR THE SAKE OF THEIR SON
The Alpha Brotherhood • Catherine Mann
They'd been the best of friends, but after one night of passion everything changed. A year later, Lucy Ann and Elliot have a baby, but is their child enough to make them a family?

#2276 BENEATH THE STETSON
Texas Cattleman's Club: The Missing Mogul
Janice Maynard
Rancher Gil Addison has few opportunities for romance, but he may have found a woman who can love him *and* his son. If only she wasn't investigating him and his club!

#2277 THE NANNY'S SECRET
Billionaires and Babies • Elizabeth Lane
Wyatt needs help when his teenager brings home a baby, but he never expects to fall for the nanny. Leigh seems almost too good to be true—until her startling revelation changes everything.

#2278 PREGNANT BY MORNING
Kat Cantrell
One magical night in Venice brings lost souls Matthew and Evangeline together. With their passionate affair inching dangerously toward something more, one positive pregnancy test threatens to drive them apart for good.

#2279 AT ODDS WITH THE HEIRESS
Las Vegas Nights • Cat Schield
Hotelier Scarlett may have inherited some dangerous secrets, but the true risk is to her heart when the man she loves to hate, security entrepreneur Logan, decides to make her safety his business.

#2280 PROJECT: RUNAWAY BRIDE
Project: Passion • Heidi Betts
Juliet can't say *I do,* so she runs out on her own wedding. But she can't hide for long when Reid, private investigator—and father of her unborn child—is on the case.

HDCNM1213

SPECIAL EXCERPT FROM

 HARLEQUIN®

Desire

Casino owner Scarlett Fontaine and
security expert Logan Wolfe
never got along, but that's all about to change in
AT ODDS WITH THE HEIRESS,
the first book in Cat Schield's new
Las Vegas Nights series…

"**D**on't you ever get tired of acting?" Logan asked, his casual tone not matching the dangerous tension emanating from him.

"What do you mean?"

"The various roles you play to fool men into accepting whatever fantasy you want them to believe. One of these days someone is going to see past your flirtation to the truth," Logan warned, his voice a husky growl.

She arched her eyebrows. "Which is what?"

"That what you need isn't some tame lapdog."

"I don't?"

"No." Espresso eyes watched her with lazy confidence. "What you need is a man who will barge right past your defenses and drive you wild."

"Don't be ridiculous," she retorted, struggling to keep her eyes off his well-shaped lips and her mind from drifting into the daydream of being kissed silly by him.

"You can lie to yourself all you want," he said. "But don't bother lying to me."

It wasn't until he captured her fingers that she realized she'd flattened her palm against his rib cage. She tugged to free her hand, but he tightened his grip.

"Let me go."

"You started it."

She wasn't completely sure that was true. "What's gotten into you today?"

He smiled. "You know, I think this is the first time I've ever seen you lose your cool. I like it."

How had he turned the tables on her in such a short time?

"I'm really not interested in what you—"

She never had a chance to finish the thought. Before she guessed his intention, Logan lowered his lips to hers and cut off her denial. Slow and deliberate, his hot mouth moved across hers.

Scarlett wanted to cry out as she experienced the delicious pleasure of his broad chest crushing her breasts, but he'd stolen her breath. Then the sound of the doors opening reached them both at the same time. Logan broke the kiss. Eyes hard and unreadable, he scrutinized her face. Scarlett felt as exposed as if she'd stepped into her casino wearing only her underwear.

Breathless, she asked, "Did that feel like acting?"

Find out what happens next in
AT ODDS WITH THE HEIRESS
by Cat Schield

Available January 2014 from Harlequin® Desire.

HDEXP1213

HARLEQUIN®

Desire

ALWAYS POWERFUL, PASSIONATE AND PROVOCATIVE.

From *USA TODAY* bestselling author
Elizabeth Lane,
a novel that asks, can desire trump deception?

Haughty and handsome, ski resort owner
Wyatt Richardson has never met a problem
he couldn't buy his way out of. Facing the
unexpected custody of his teenage daughter
and her newborn son, he swiftly hires a nanny to
handle them both. His attraction to Leigh Foster
is an unexpected perk. He's confident the feeling
is mutual.

Leigh knows she is on shaky ground. Falling for
her new employer could prove devastating—
especially if Wyatt finds out her true connection
to baby Mikey. But when the billionaire's strong
arms beckon, will she be powerless to refuse?

Look for
THE NANNY'S SECRET
next month, from Harlequin Desire!

Wherever books and ebooks are sold.

HD73290

HARLEQUIN®

Desire

ALWAYS POWERFUL, PASSIONATE AND PROVOCATIVE.

Wanted distractions in Royal, Texas

Being a single dad is millionaire rancher Gil Addison's number one pastime. But when state investigator Bailey Collins comes to Royal, Texas, he can't ignore the woman beneath the badge. Bailey is hot on the heels of a kidnapper in Gil's Cattleman's Club and won't stop until she has her man in cuffs. Only problem being, straitlaced Bailey finds herself distracted by thoughts of the sexy rancher, who is on a mission of his own—to get Bailey into bed.

Look for BENEATH THE STETSON next month,
from Harlequin Desire!

Don't miss other scandalous titles from the
TEXAS CATTLEMAN'S CLUB miniseries,
available now wherever books and ebooks are sold.

Powerful heroes…scandalous secrets…burning desires.

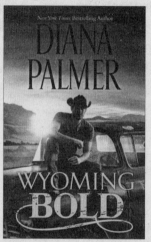